The Sword Above Us

Leigh Fields

Contents

For those of us who are too used to a cage,
be free.   '

Chapter One

Zale

"D rown."

I released the fury of the sea that filled my veins. The water swelled in like a tsunami, fast and deadly. I stared directly into the silver eyes of my soulmate and willed his life away. His dark magic swirled around him and carried him away from my waters.

At least he was gone.

The gold markings across my skin faded as magic settled in my chest again. The mansion lay in ruins, with only the raised platform remaining. My coronation dress was drenched and clung to my legs. My crown tilted off center on my head, so I snatched it and tossed it aside.

I was glad to be rid of this place.

"Zale."

"It's *High Queen*," I snapped.

"Forgive me," my dearest friend dipped his head to me. "High Queen, we must go."

I pushed the dark waves from my face and focused on myself—deep breaths in and out, like a breeze across the sea.

"High Queen, we must go to Firestorm. The Dragon King could return any moment—"

"The Dragon King is not a concern. He will not return until he is sure he can win. I have business in New Orleans, not Firestorm." I turned to leave the slab of concrete—all that was left of the mansion—but Lance blocked my way.

"My queen, forgive me, but we must go." His dark eyes glared at me, and I glowered back at him.

"Do not stand in my way."

"I'm tasked with keeping you safe."

"I can handle my own safety."

"Zale, please. We just watched him destroy the entire royal family days ago." My friend's pleading look was the only thing that stopped me. I held up my hand while the other gripped my sopping skirt.

"I am going to New Orleans. If you must accompany me, I won't object. Once my business there is done, I will go to Firestorm as you suggest. But, Lance, you cannot contain me. No one can. It is not in the nature of the sea to be contained."

Twenty-eight years ago...

A hand covered my mouth in the darkness. My eyelids shot open and I could almost make out the deep blue orbs of my aunt's eyes. She held a finger to her lips, signaling me to remain quiet. I nodded, and she took my hand before dragging me out of bed.

I trusted my aunt, so I didn't question her strange behavior. Keani might be wild, even by dragon standards, but she was loyal. She handed me a white dress and motioned for me to put it on, then led me down several passages and out onto the beach under the full moon. The waves were angry and forceful beneath the soft light. She dragged me to the water's edge before I finally freed my hand and stopped.

"Keani, what are we doing here?"

"Come, Zale, there isn't much time," she whispered before reaching for my hand again.

I pulled away. "Tell me what's happening," I demanded. My trust only went so far.

She sighed and placed a hand on her enlarged abdomen. "My time is almost up. There is no other way," she said cryptically as she looked out over the ocean.

"I don't understand." I remained firm.

Keani snatched my arm and dragged me out into the surf. "What I'm about to tell you has to remain a secret. Only the High King knows this, but I wouldn't trust him moving forward, if I were you. Even he cannot know."

The waves crashed around my thighs, and she turned us to face each other in the ocean.

"The ocean has chosen you, and I agree," she continued. "The Heart of the Sea resides in me, and now I will pass it to you."

My eyes widened, and I felt the blood drain from my face. "What? No, I don't understand. That magic is sacred. It resides in the stone with the High King."

She gave me an unreadable look. "The sea gives her magic to whom she chooses. Long ago, she chose me. My time is almost up, and now she has chosen you."

I shook my head. "No, Keani. I'm not strong enough. My father..."

Her face turned to stone. "Your father knows nothing. You were the only good contribution he has ever brought to the Sea clan."

Tears fell down my face, and I shook my head more vigorously. "But what about your child? Surely, they will have your strength. They will be a better fit for this."

Keani placed her hand under my chin and lifted my face to see hers. "The sea has chosen you. Deep Magic runs in your veins. My child will have more than enough dangers to face on her own. Now give me your hand. We are running out of time."

I looked at Keani's outstretched hand. My aunt had always loved and cared for me. She had never led me astray. My hand shook, but I put it in hers and waited. The waves became more powerful and crashed around us, but Keani stood firm, even with her rounded belly weighing her down.

Blue flames wound down her arms from her chest, and they connected to mine, calling forth my magic. Two spirals of fire that looked like waves in the ocean moved like a whirlpool on her chest. After a moment, a blue stone formed and came up from beneath her skin. I tried to pull away from Keani, but she held me firm.

The stone passed the distance between us until it settled in my chest. I was overwhelmed by the magic. Powerful, calming, but wild magic poured into my chest and limbs till I was full to the brim. When I thought I couldn't take anymore, a wave crashed over me, and the world went black.

I awoke in my bed, convinced it was all a dream. That was until I saw the single piece of paper next to my bed. "Tell no one," was all it read.

Chapter Two

Zale

"Burn it?" Lance looked at me as if I did not give him a direct order to destroy my grandfather's estate.

"Burn it."

"Zale, it is only a house. It cannot hurt you."

I stared at him, holding my chin high.

"I believe I gave you a direct order."

"High Queen," Lance's tone became formal once more. "Perhaps you would like to walk the estate before we destroy it. There may be something that you do not want to see burn."

"Speak plainly, Lance. I don't need riddles. As you have pointed out at least a dozen times, we are on a timeline."

Lance turned to Nyla. "Want to take it from here?"

My friend raised her hands in the air and stepped away from us. "I have no reason to ignore the queen's order."

My lips twitched toward a smile, but I spent much of my life remaining as still as a statue, so it did not break. Lance moved in front of me again and touched my shoulders. He ducked his broad frame so we were eye to eye. "Be at peace with this place, my queen. There is no reason the past should haunt you now."

Lance straightened and then pulled me forward to his chest. He kissed my temple before releasing me and stepping back. I swallowed down the emotions, although they all beckoned me to dive into their depths. Now was neither the time nor the place.

I reached my hand for Nyla and she clasped it, joining me at my side. Her strength was appreciated. Years, she and Lance stood at my side while I worked secretly to free the dragons enslaved to the Shadows. They witnessed the atrocities committed against me in childhood and in recent months. If they were asking me to face my demons, perhaps I should.

Hand in hand, we climbed the stairs to the mansion where my grandfather, the former High King, had resided with my mother and father. No fondness found me here. No warm memories or comfort lived in these walls.

"You don't have to do this, Zay," Nyla said. "I don't care what Lance says. You're the queen now."

I squeezed her hand. "He's right. Let me face these memories and be done with this place."

"Fine." My friend straightened herself and faced the doors. "Where do you want to start?"

"The dungeon."

"Dive right in, don't you?"

I gave a small smile to her for that. "I don't do anything lightly. I'm all in, and you know it."

"Come on then. Let's not keep those demons waiting."

Nyla and I moved through the mansion and down the damp steps to the dungeon below. Unusual for New Orleans to have any building underground, but somehow the High King managed it. I gripped the iron on the heavy wooden door and pushed it open.

A small gasp came from the dragon beside me. She knew my story, unlike most, but the shock of seeing it cannot compare to hearing it secondhand. Before us were my typical quarters whenever my father and grandfather felt the need to "prevent my wanderings."

Tools of pain lined the wall, and I ran my hand over each of them. The cattle prod was my father's favorite. The whip, the iron screws meant to crush, and blades of all forms greeted me like old friends. Long ago, I came to terms with each of them. The royal family could abuse and mutilate this body, but my will was my own.

"You were a princess. A royal. How could..." Nyla drifted off as she stepped further into the dungeon.

"It was never about me. It was about the image the High King needed to maintain and that my father wished for me to show. They believed it would keep the clan united and prevent factions from forming. Their precious heiress could not be seen dissenting against our laws, saving enslaved dragons, or wandering the seas. The heiress must be the embodiment of the Sea clan. She must carry on the Silva family name and power."

The words bounced around my head, with my father's voice echoing behind them. He screamed those words at me often. I would have killed him long ago if he had not been joined with my mother.

In a wave of fury, I swiped my hands across the wall where the tools rested. They clattered to the floor and, while it eased the fire in my chest, it was not enough. Blue fire spiraled around my arms in response to my emotions, a flaw, and I reeled the magic in quickly.

"Enough of this, Zay. What else do you need to see? Let us be done with this place," Nyla insisted.

Turning on my heels, I flipped my hair over my shoulder and headed back up the stairs. I needed to see only one other place—Ada's room.

My feet knew the way, and I plotted my destruction of this place with every step. My imprisonment became nearly unbearable weeks earlier when the High King realized I would not prophesy where the Heart of the Sea resided.

The sea frequently shifted, as she was ever-changing, but her depths ran in my veins. Her secrets demanded to remain locked in my chest. And so the High King became more frustrated at the lack of respect and abused this body. He relied on my father to carry on when he was predisposed.

My mother's face on the night of her death made it clear that she had no part to play in my suffering. Would it be different had she known? I shook the thought from my mind. It did not matter.

What I needed from her was information. As my aunt's sister, she was the closest to her. A new threat was looming these last months, an ethereal voice calling from the north. *Wander*, it called to me. No one else seemed to hear it, but strange magic was nothing new to me.

Nyla followed me to my mother's room. The deep blues that covered the bed and the walls were her favorite, and she couldn't resist pairing them with the gold trim. A tugging in my heart asked me to use my magic, but I ignored it. My grief needed to wait. The need to answer the strange voice threatened to distract me from my task to lead the Sea clan against the Shadow dragons.

"Somewhere here is a purple journal. I need that," I explained to Nyla.

She nodded and moved to my mother's desk. I scanned the room and pondered where she would keep such a treasure. Keani's journal would be desired by more than myself. What would my clever mother do?

My eyes landed on a bookshelf. Surely it couldn't be that obvious. Could it?

I ran to the books and pulled each of them off the shelf, removing their covers and tossing them over my shoulder. About a third of the way through the second shelf, I discovered a second copy of Jane Eyre. I tore the cover, and beneath it was the purple journal I remember from my childhood. Keani's name was written in the bottom front corner.

"I've got it."

"Great! Let's get out of here!" Nyla sped to my side and linked her arm with mine. I allowed her to drag me out of the house.

Lance's eyes searched out mine as we descended the steps. I nodded to him, a silent thank you for the push to walk through my troubles. Plenty was before us, and leaving as many behind as possible was best. Now was the time to cleanse this place with fire and water.

With my closest friends, I lit up my past and watched the infernal family mansion burn to the ground.

Chapter Three

Zale

"High Queen, you cannot leave! We need to get you up to speed before you meet with the Mountain Queen."

I continued walking past the advisor who had no business trying to advise me. "Do I look like I need to be brought up to speed?"

"There are delicate matters involving the relationship between the clans."

I spun on the slim dragon that followed me down the corridor. "I do not need to be prattled to like a child. I am your High Queen. The Mountain Queen is my cousin. I'm well aware of the state of affairs."

The dragon backed away but continued making his point. "But the Mountain Queen is a rogue. She has a claim to your throne."

"She renounced her claim to my throne. You know this. Why are you bringing it up? I don't have time for this."

I would have waited for his answer if I were a kinder dragon. Kindness hardly had a place for me as the High Queen of our clan.

Lance walked toward me and held his hand up to stop the incompetent advisor behind me. I continued past him down the narrow hall. He caught up and took my elbow, guiding me to my private study. "Is it necessary to be unkind to every advisor from Sea clan? They are *your* clan."

"They are also snakes. Do you think I don't know who was whispering in my father's ear? My grandfather's?"

In the quiet of privacy, Lance pulled me into his arms and I leaned against his chest. He held me close and ran his hand over my hair. "You are better than them. You don't have to let the world burn with your anger."

I pulled away from my friend. "Lance, you know that I can find their sins and secrets. I can bring them to their knees. The only reason they are still here is because I allow it. I am *allowing* these advisors a chance."

He raised his brow. "Does a chance look like what I just saw, Zale?"

Ice dripped down my spine at his words. My shoulders tensed, and I held perfectly still as my eyes darted to his face.

"Zale." Lance reached for me again. Without another thought, I called the deep magic to the surface—my gold tattoos flickered on my skin, attempting to hold it in check.

"Don't," I whispered.

Lance paused and his eyes scanned my body. "Zay." He raised his hands in surrender. "I won't touch you."

Blue flames filled my vision. No matter how slowly or deeply I breathed, the magic consumed me, attempting to divert a threat that did not exist.

"Zay, you're safe. There is no one here that can harm you."

"I'm not safe," I said through gritted teeth, a breath away from shifting.

"You can protect yourself. There is no one here that can challenge you. No one with the extent of your power here."

Not here. There was one whose power could exceed mine.

"Zay, the house is shaking. If you plan to call the sea here to destroy us all, I ask you not to. Please."

Lance's voice was calm and even, never betraying the anxiety I was sure he held at my display of power. I ran my hand over my arm, begging the deep magic to subside. Biting my lip, I willed the gold tattoos to fade, their purpose served.

I locked eyes with my friend and he frowned. "What triggered you this time? Do you know?"

I turned my back to him and laid my hands on the desk, bending over it to catch my breath. "I know you did not mean it this way, but Leo would ask condescending questions before he struck me. Every time. It was part of his method."

"I'm sorry, Zay. I'm so sorry."

I spun and faced him. "I don't want your pity. That was part of my past."

"Zay."

"No, Lance. I am the High Queen. If I am to lead this clan, it must stay in the past. We are on the brink of war. My scars will stay in the past, where they belong."

Lance backed away from me and spread his arms. "As you wish, my queen, but remember that no matter how deep you bury them, you still carry your demons until you face them."

He exited through the door. He wouldn't leave. Lance was never far when I was in need. If God were kinder, he would have been my soulmate—the calm to my storm. But that was not my story. And he was not my soulmate.

Sleep would help me, but I didn't want to dream tonight. The prophetic magic waited for my mind to still, hovering like a sword above my head, ready to drop.

I brought my hands to my face and scrubbed the weariness from my eyes. I needed to review the notes Nyla had left before meeting with Jenna. When I reached for the notes on my desk, something out of place caught my attention.

A tan envelope with a black seal rested on top of the papers. The seal held the emblem of a sword with a dragon curled around it.

I recognized that seal from my dreams.

The seal of the Dragon King.

Chapter Four

Zale

*M*y treasured soulmate,

    How long do you think I will allow you to hide from me? You may be allowed more freedom than I give to others, but my leniency only goes so far. I will have you by my side. Soon.

    I have entertained your futile attempts to evade me and undermine me long enough. If I do not have you with me by the end of the year, I will take more drastic measures. I am giving you a chance to come to me of your own free will. The choice is yours.

    Sincerely,

    Your King, Axel

I lit the parchment on fire in my hand and scanned my room for any sign he was still there. How did he find me? Was that part of his plan? To unsettle me?

It wasn't likely to work.

I was the High Queen.

No sign of the Dragon King remained. His letter was the only clue that he had been there at all. Pulling in a breath, I marched out of the room to where Lance stood at the door.

"Search the room."

"Your Majesty?"

"Search it. The Dragon King was here."

Lance's eyes darkened and he moved swiftly into my room. I did not need him to search it, but keeping up the charade that I needed protection had kept me hidden for many years. Lance returned and put his hands on my face, scanning my eyes. He looked as if he was about to speak, but he pulled me into his chest instead.

"I'm not harmed." I pulled away and straightened myself.

"It was too close for comfort. Please. Let's go to Firestorm."

"I need to meet with Jenna. Then we may go as you insist."

"Zay, please don't delay."

Lance placed his hand on my cheek. His touch was as familiar as my own. Time stood still, and we were frozen in the moment. His eyes dipped to my mouth before his lips connected with mine. I wrapped my arm around his neck and pulled him closer. He coaxed my lips apart, deepening our kiss.

A tear trickled down my cheek. We both knew this would only lead to heartbreak, but I kissed him with everything in me. I loved him. My faithful friend. My confidant.

I pulled back with a heavy heart and turned to face away from him.

"This is not fair to you."

Lance ran his hands down my arms. "I can decide what is fair to me."

"You know this only makes you a target."

He snaked his hand around my waist and pulled my back flush with his front. Tilting his head down, he whispered. "I do not fear death. I do not fear this king you say is bonded to you. You deserve so much better than a dragon that enslaves his own."

"Do not ask me to walk down this road with you. I have seen the end...and I cannot bear your death on my conscience."

Lance placed gentle kisses along my neck and temple. "As you wish, my queen."

The calming touch at my back retreated, and the door shut softly as he left. I pulled my hands over my face and allowed a few more tears for my broken heart.

Alone. That was what it meant to walk my path.

The world owed me a debt for this and so much more.

A sound from my phone filled the room. One that only belonged to Nyla.

I opened the desk drawer and answered the phone that rested inside. "Where?"

"I can bring them to you."

"How many?"

"Three."

"Are you close?"

"Tomorrow night. Can you stay in New Orleans one more day?"

It would be difficult to convince the advisors, but this was important. "Yes. Nyla, what will we do once we are in Firestorm?"

"My queen, it is up to you. I'll bring them wherever you tell me."

"I will see you tomorrow."

I ended the call and slid the phone back into the desk drawer. And not a moment too soon. The advisor, whose name I refused to learn, entered my suite.

"The Mountain Queen has arrived."

"I will not be summoned like a dog. Leave. I will greet my cousin when I am able."

The advisor opened his mouth to speak again. I sent a spiral of blue flames into his chest, and he collapsed against the wall. I picked up a pair of gold cuffs off the desk and clicked them in place before pulling the dragon by his arm. I dragged him in his stupor to the main room. He stumbled often, and I pulled him upright each time.

The doors stood between me and the rest of my advisors. I threw my fire into them, sending them flying off their hinges.

Silence filled the air. All eyes locked on me.

Holding my chin high, I dragged the dragon into the middle of the room and deposited him on the floor.

I nodded to Jenna. "Forgive me, Mountain Queen. I have a matter to attend to before we begin our meeting."

The Sea clan wanted a ruthless queen, and so they would have her. I took my seat at the center of the table along the wall. With my fingers interlaced, I leaned onto the table.

"You will not use me like a puppet. I am your High Queen. Disrespect from this moment forward will be punishable by death or exile."

"Your Majesty, our job is—"

"Your job," my voice cut through the dragon's words like a sword. "Your job is to advise. I am to lead. The first thing you must wrap your arrogant minds around is that if we are going to deal with the Shadows, we will need allies."

A murmur rose from the dragons. I expected as much. They were unused to looking outside of their own ambitions. This was one reason that I was shut away so often in the past.

Dragons did not need to be divided. My dreams prophesied a time when there were no clans—a future where dragons were strong and fruitful.

But fear and prejudice, and selfish desires stood in the way of that future.

So did a Dragon King, but one problem at a time.

"I am no longer in need of your advice. I will speak to my cousin alone."

I waited for them to challenge me. Surely, at least one Sea dragon in the room did not want to be told what to do. But one by one, they each left until no one but Lance and the Mountain Dragons remained.

"What would you like me to do with this one?"

Lance pulled the unfortunate advisor I had deposited on the floor to his feet.

"Take him to one of the rooms. He can recover there."

Lance nodded before removing the advisor.

Jenna and Kipp stood side by side. Finally, when we were alone, a grin spread on my cousin's face.

"Well, that was quite the show." Jenna wrapped her arms around me. Her familiarity after these last years still unsettled me. I patted her back until she released me.

Her blue eyes reminded me so much of Ada's and my heart ached for my mother. I would trade so many things to have her at my side. Or even Keani and her strange ways.

Jenna's eyes flashed with dangerous white flames as she spoke. "So tell me, what did you have in mind for taking on the Shadows? They have something of mine, and I want it back."

Chapter Five

Zale

I sat back in my seat and grinned at her. "We wait."

"Wait?"

"Yes. We wait."

"That's hardly a plan." Jenna crossed her arms over her chest and raised a brow.

"It is. He wants something I have. The Dragon King will come to me."

Kipp moved closer to the table. "Here?"

"No. I'll draw him to Firestorm."

Jenna sat across from me, and Kipp joined her at the table. "Can the fortress handle an attack of that force?"

"It can. I'm hoping you will join me there."

Jenna shared a look with Kipp. "I can't leave the clan or my family. They're vulnerable now that the Capitol is destroyed."

I reached my hand across the table and touched her arm. "Jenna. Bring them. All of them."

Her blue eyes bounced from my touch to my face. "You really think this is a good idea?"

Pulling my hand back, I interlaced my fingers and laid them on the table. "It's time. We cannot hope to defeat the Dragon King or his Shadows separately."

"I agree, but I don't think that fighting among ourselves will be helpful either," Kipp said.

I tilted my head to Jenna. "Do you think you can keep your clan in check?"

She eyed me with suspicion. "I think it is your clan you need to worry about, cousin."

"I am more than capable of managing my clan. Can we agree on rules for cohabitation?"

"You're serious?"

"Very."

My cousin shared a look with her soulmate. Love and respect radiated from them. It was hard not to envy their bond. I pushed the thought of soulmates away. I already knew Jenna would take my deal. My dreams had shown it, but I waited for her to answer.

"What rules did you have in mind, High Queen?"

One hurdle down. I smiled. "No murder, no stealing, no fighting."

Kipp scoffed. "You think it will be that simple."

"On punishment of death or exile? Yes, I believe it will be that simple."

"And what of humans?" Jenna's face hardened. "The Shadows aren't simply going to ignore them. How will we protect them?"

"I don't expect them to. Keep your spies where they are, but bring the bulk of your clan to me. Keep his eyes on me."

It was hard to be patient when I knew what she would say next. "Zale, you are his soulmate. Did you know this?"

"Yes. I have known for some time."

The weight of that knowledge settled in the room.

"Soulmates make things tricky, cousin."

Flashes of blue in my vision warned me not to respond quickly. My magic burned hot and begged to be released. I breathed deeply and suppressed the flames before answering. "This is my destiny. I was born to play this game."

Kipp leaned forward. "What do you know?"

"He walks on the edge of a sword. The slightest tilt in either direction will mean the end of magic for all dragons. The future is uncertain. Simeon saw to that."

"How, Zale? How do you know?"

I closed my eyes. There was no reason to hide it from her any longer. The gold tattoos flared to life as my magic surged like the tide. Blue flames spiraled down my arms and hovered in my hands. When I opened my eyes, Jenna rose to her feet.

"I've not shared with you the extent of my magic."

"Why?"

"It was not safe. He was looking for me. You know as much as anyone how a soulmate can change a dragon. And I carry the Heart of the Sea. He could not know."

"The Dragon King?"

I nodded. "To balance the bonds of soulmates, my magic is from the deep parts of the sea. I have to be able to match my soulmate's capacity."

"His *capacity*? Shit, are you saying he holds even more power? I know he is a rogue. His white flames at your ceremony proved that."

"I do not know his story, but my visions show he is beyond any other dragon known."

"Visions?"

"Prophecy. Part of the deep magic."

She narrowed her eyes. "What do you know? What have you seen?"

"Many things." Jenna didn't need to know everything. I let the magic settle back under my skin—the need to show my magic was no longer necessary.

"My parents?"

I swallowed. Keani often spoke to me in my dreams. "I see many things, but only pieces. I rarely have the full picture."

Kipp laid his hand on Jenna's shoulder. "Sunshine," he murmured. He faced me again. "What of the Dragon King?"

"My visions were clear before Simeon joined his soulmate."

"How did that change the future?"

"Before, the visions showed a clear defeat of the Shadows and the Dragon King. Whatever he did, it rewrote what was meant to be. Now the future is...unclear at best."

"Unclear?"

"Dragons will either succumb to the Shadows or cease to exist."

"Those cannot be the only options." I adored Jenna and her stubborn resolve, but she pushed where she should not.

"I'm trying to avoid those options. I'm looking for a second prophecy."

Kipp leaned close. "What does this second prophecy have to do with Mountain clan?"

"The second prophecy described salvation. I need to find it."

"You have given me much to think about, cousin. I will return to our clan and notify you of our decision."

"Are you not their queen, Jenna?"

Her eyes flashed white. "I do not choose to rule as you do. I will discuss this with the families and notify you of our decision."

I hated to push her away, but the further away she was from me, emotionally, the better for all involved. Her humanity demanded family connection, but we were dragons, not humans. And if my visions were correct, she would need to be able to separate the two before this war was done.

I watched Kipp and Jenna pass through the portal before returning to my study. It was time I found that pesky second prophecy and read it for myself. I lifted the purple journal with Keani's name on it and sat at the desk to find my fate.

Chapter Six

Zale

My fingers trembled as I opened the pages. In my dreams, Keani had urged me to find it. Why she did not tell me herself made no sense. She wrote the prophecy.

The handwriting was hardly legible, and some of it was in old script, but the Heart of the Sea made it easier to read. Simeon had distracted me too many times when Mother wanted to teach it to us in our youth. Thankfully, the strange stone that lived in my chest unscrambled the letters in my mind.

For hours, I scanned the pages of Keani's journal until I found something strange.

Black ink filled the page, the same three stanzas written over and over again. That was odd enough, but more so was the maroon that traced each letter, feathering out to various shades as if she had written over it many times. I brushed my fingers over the page and felt the deep grooves where Keani had pressed her pen into the letters. She had been tracing them in blood.

It had to be the prophecy. I took a deep breath and forced myself to read the words I had been searching for.

Oceans are frozen deep
Remember the tides
Mountains will crumble

Fires will rise

Hiding in silence

The Shadows are alive

All roads point to this time

Use the sword to survive

The King is coming

His time has arrived

I read the words over and over again before ripping the page from the journal and clutching it tight. This was the prophecy?

We were truly doomed.

Sleep tugged at my mind, but I wasn't ready to face her yet. Keani rarely spoke plainly, and my mind was weary from all the recent events. I wasn't sure I could decipher what she was telling me just yet. I needed to rest first.

I stood and replaced the journal in the drawer. I changed and settled in the bed, leaving the light on, as was my habit. Easier to see the Shadows that way.

Clutching the page from my aunt's journal, I stared at the ceiling as my chest began to throb. I rubbed the area that held the stone, hoping that it would cease. But if history was any indication, I would not rest tonight.

My mind drifted in a fog to the space between sleeping and waking.

I stood on the beach while the sun beat down on my skin. I scanned up and down the coast until I saw her. The one who called me to this "in-between" as she named it. She faced the ocean, and the wind blew back her blond hair.

As I approached, her eyes opened and glanced in my direction. "I've been waiting a while, Zale."

"It was not easy to find. Why did you not tell me yourself?"

Keani faced me, and her fierce blue eyes bore into me. "I've told you before. I fight to be here. To guide you. My spirit demands rest."

"Why do you insist on calling me here? Let your spirit rest, Keani."

She turned her head out toward the sea and inhaled deeply. "Foolish child. The world hangs in the balance. Your king walks on the edge of the sword, and the slightest tilt one way or the other will mean every dragon perishes."

My jaw clenched. "He is not my king. I am the High Queen now. I answer to no one."

Keani stroked my cheek. "He is everyone's king."

I turned away from my aunt. Her words hardly ever made sense, even in life. In death, her logic was...flawed. "You told me that he would be destroyed."

"That time has passed."

"How? The only thing that changed was Simeon's rescue of his soulmate. Surely that didn't upset the balance."

Keani's face grew stern. "The pale rogue and his mate were to perish. Their magic returned to the clans. The stars wrote this. You saw this."

Her words were an accusation—one that was true. I saw his death in the stars, and so I remained silent.

"You healed him of the Shadows."

Another allegation, but I didn't let this one slip by without a rebuttal.

"I did. He is my family. Would you ask me to lose them all?"

"You have your clan. You have Jenna. It was selfish, Zale."

Blue flames spiraled down my arm and the gold on my flesh flashed to life. "I made a choice. One I do not regret. I choose to have him at my side. You can say I've lost my mind, but if I'm going to build this empire and take on the Shadows, I need all the power I can find at my disposal."

Keani lifted a single brow. "You would use your magic here? I am but a ghost."

"Enough of your chastising, Keani. Tell me what the prophecy means. Tell me what I need to know."

I thrust the page from her journal into her hand. She stared over it, confusion marring her face. Her eyes filled with a haze as she stared out over the ocean, deep in thought. After the waves crashed for many moments around us, she blinked and her face pinched. "I do not remember writing these words."

"What of the sword? The king? Please remember something."

"Child, I wrote many prophecies in my life. Some were clear and came to pass quickly. Some were foggy and have never happened. I do not remember."

"You said this would be our salvation, that this prophecy was the one to show me the way. Please."

Keani stroked my cheek, and her hair flowed behind her in the breeze. "For your sake, I wish I could remember, but I do not. Our time is nearly done."

"What am I to do, Keani?"

She dropped her hand. "You are the High Queen, bearer of the Heart of the Sea, soulmate to the Dragon King. You will know what to do when the time comes. Trust your instincts."

I flinched at the mention of soulmates. This information often haunted my mind. I had known for some time, but there were no easy answers. He remained my enemy as long as he continued to poison dragons with the Shadows.

My eyes blinked open, and I stared at the ceiling, reorienting myself. My mind snapped like a bowstring whenever I was pulled from these visions.

It was too dark—I had left the light on when I went to sleep.

Sitting straight up, I let the blue flames lick down my arms and light my vision.

There, leaning against my desk, stood the Dragon King. He played white flames along his fingers, and they lit his face with ghastly shadows—a wicked smirk formed on his face.

"Hello, princess. Did you get my letter?"

Chapter Seven

Zale

I didn't hesitate when I saw him leaning comfortably against the desk. I swept the covers back and stood beside my bed. The gold rose on my skin and lit the room around us as the stone thrummed to life in my chest.

Blue flames from my hands careened into his palm as he caught the fire. Only a twitch of his lip betrayed that he was displeased.

"You have no right to be here. Leave, or I will call the ocean to my aid again," I demanded.

You have no right to make demands of your king, princess.

His words echoed in my mind even though his lips never once moved.

I narrowed my eyes. That was new. *Get out of my head.*

The Dragon King laughed. "You have something of mine. If I remember correctly, you made a deal, and I am owed the Heart of the Sea."

"You possessed it for a time. It is not my fault you did not hold on to it."

He stepped closer and my flames flashed brighter. I kept my eyes on him but scanned my room in my peripheral vision. He was alone.

Rather, we were alone.

"I'll be certain not to make the same mistake twice." The king—Axel, looked me up and down as if assessing a target. He was not my king, so I would refer to him by name.

"I doubt you will have the chance a second time."

Silence filled the space between us. I watched him intently, waiting for him to begin whatever game he was playing this time. He tilted his head as he spoke. "You are...not what I was expecting."

Axel stepped toward me again. I allowed him to come closer. He could get as close as he wanted. The impact of my flames would only be that much more powerful.

I tipped my chin up to see his face as he stepped close enough to touch me. His silver eyes flashed white, but the flames did not go down his arms, so I waited. My magic thrummed, and my heart beat loudly in response to his closeness. He reached into the space between us and clenched his fist. I could not see the golden cord between us, but I knew it was there. The touch was harsh and abrasive on my soul, but it sent a bolt of ice through to the edges of my fingers, like diving into cold waters.

Enough. I sent blue flames into his chest, pushing Axel away. He may be my soulmate, but he did not have any authority over me.

He dropped his hand and my breath hitched. I wasn't sure if it was relief or regret, but he wasn't close, and I could think more clearly. Axel straightened, tugged on the sleeves of his suit, and ran a hand down his dress shirt.

"I have a problem," he began.

I scoffed. "You have many problems."

His brow raised slightly. "We have a mutual problem. Neither of us wants this cord. I have tried severing it, but it is unlike most cords."

"You have cut cords?" Bile climbed the back of my throat. Who would do such a thing? "What ties you to your magic? Your family?"

Axel ignored my questions. "This cord is a thick—a binding tether which does not yield to most magic."

When he didn't continue, I narrowed my eyes. "What do you want me to do about it? You're right. I don't want this. I didn't ask for this."

Axel began to pace toward the window, and I pivoted to match his steps. "*I* cannot sever the cord, but you, dear soulmate, might be able to do it."

His words sent shivers up my spine and ice through my veins. Sever the cord? Did I dare to hope? I narrowed my eyes. "Why are you here, Axel?"

He stopped and raised an eyebrow. "I already told you why I am here."

I clenched my hands at my sides, bracing for the impact of my words. He would not be pleased with my response. "Then you came for nothing. I will not surrender the Heart of the Sea, and I have no way to sever cords. I can't even see them. Now, I did not invite you here. Leave."

White flames flashed in his eyes. "You do not get to call the shots, princess. I will have the stone one way or another."

My senses prickled as Axel's magic began to surface, and my body thrummed with the force of my magic combined with the stone. I allowed the blue flames to consume my body. The Heart of the Sea pulsed, causing me to hover on the edge of shifting, my dragon begging to be released.

Axel laughed. "If you shift, you don't stand a chance. Your clan doesn't stand a chance against me."

"I don't need to shift to make you leave." Raising my hands, I released the full force of my magic into his chest. He caught the flames, as I expected. A part of me enjoyed seeing him entirely focused on my flames. His arms held steady and white flames began to push back against my magic. It was almost too easy. I smiled as the gold tattoos lifted from my skin and hovered in the air. I increased the intensity of my fire, and the ocean answered my call. Waves broke through the walls and windows of my suite. The water swirled around my target before engulfing him in the saltwater.

Axel's white flames disappeared, and dark magic slid around him. His eyes flashed white again, and he winked before disappearing into the Shadows.

I released my grip on the sea and the waves retreated. My gold tattoos settled back in my skin as my breath heaved in my chest. I leaned over the edge of the bed and screamed. The commotion on the other side of my suite door would have to wait.

I let my flames consume the bed and screamed again. How could I be so foolish?

Angry tears slid down my face. I let my clan down. My strategy relied heavily on the secrets I kept.

Familiar hands gripped my shoulders and turned me into an embrace. Lance.

He ran his hand down my hair as he spoke—his tone soothing and calm. I couldn't meet his gaze, and I couldn't make my voice work. If I did, I would lose control completely, and that would be worse than the mistake I had only just made.

There was only one reason Axel was here, and I played right into his hand.

He was here to see the extent of my powers.

Chapter Eight

Zale

*W*ander.

The voice called at the most inconvenient times. I pushed the strange calling from my mind.

"Why do you insist on staying until everyone has moved? You are the one he wants. We need to get you to Firestorm."

I rubbed my temples and opened my eyes to see Lance's worried face. I reached out and touched his cheek.

"It is because he is looking for me that I must stay. I will stay here until our defenses are secure and our clan is safe behind the walls."

"Zay, this is madness. He was here. Here in this very room. What if he had overpowered you?"

I dropped my hand. "Do you not trust your queen?"

"I worry for my queen. She is playing a dangerous game."

I crossed my arms over my chest and rose to my feet. "Lance. This is where I remain for now. Take our clan to Firestorm."

"Here? Here where there are no more windows and walls because you called the sea to your aid? Here where he stood and challenged you in this very room? You are asking too much of me. I can't leave you here unprotected."

His words rubbed against my nerves. I didn't need his protection. I never did, but he did not know that. I drew in a breath and released it as I offered a solution.

"What if I bring my brother here? Will that make it easier for you to do as your queen asks?"

Lance crossed his arms over his chest. "You would rely on the rogue for your protection?"

"Enough. He is my brother. He will come if I ask. He has sworn his allegiance to me."

"Simeon is a trickster. He will not keep his word."

"He will to me."

"You don't know this. You cannot know the future."

"I do know this!" I moved closer to him, willing him to understand as my frustration and anger grew. "I have seen it. I *do* see the future. Do you not understand the extent of my power, even after all this time as my friend?"

My words slapped Lance as flames flashed dangerously around my body. He narrowed his eyes before dipping his head to acknowledge my power. After I cooled the fire around me, he dropped his hands to his side and closed the distance between us. "Is that all we are? Friends?"

His closeness brought comfort to my mind, but his words stirred up my heart. Why did he ask this of me? He knew my choices. He knew my circumstances, and yet he still asked.

"I wish it were different. Truly, I do." It hurt to say the words because they were true.

He touched my face, gently pushing back my hair. "You have a choice."

I did not respond. He had asked an unspoken question. One I would not answer. Lance's face hardened before he turned and stormed out of my study, speaking over his shoulder as he left. "Call your rogue. I will gather the clan as you wish, High Queen."

Wander.

That damn voice continued its call all day, increasing the pressure in my mind. Ever since I had awoken that morning, it had haunted me.

I turned my thoughts to Axel and my plan.

My plan was a good one. I would stay here in New Orleans until the clan settled in Firestorm, then Mountain clan would join us there. Firestorm provided enormous safety from the Shadows. The enchanted island could not be accessed except with Sea clan magic. From there, we would fight. From there, we would rescue the dragons from the Shadows. From Firestorm, I would see the Dragon King overturned.

I hated this plan.

Why was I restricting myself to a cage? In my mind, my dragon roared against the idea. Axel already knew the extent of my power. What point was there in keeping secrets?

We had lived in a prison for too long, my dragon and I. Enough was enough.

A beating drum echoed in my mind until I realized it was my heart. I lifted my hands and blue flames spiraled down my arms while gold hovered close above my skin. Heat burned in my veins, and my skin tingled with the promise of shifting. My dragon begged to be set free, clawing at my chest just below the surface.

Was I not the High Queen? Didn't the Heart of the Sea reside in my chest? What did I have to fear?

Nyla would be here soon with those enslaved to the Shadows. Until then, who would stop me?

I pushed my doors open with such force they slammed against the mansion's walls. I was bombarded with advisors and dragons calling for my attention as soon as I left my suite. I ignored each of them. The sea called me. My dragon called me.

My feet carried me with certainty down to the sand. I stripped off my shoes and ran the last feet into the waves. The moment my feet hit the water, warmth flooded me and I vibrated with magic.

"High Queen!"

I turned in the waves, the surf lapping at my thighs. Lance stood on the beach with several advisors. He scowled as he approached me in the waves.

"High Queen. You shouldn't be here alone."

I wanted to rebuke him, but another swell of the tide grabbed my attention. I grinned at him before laughing at the sky.

"Stop! Zale, no!"

I turned and dove beneath the surface, allowing my dragon to pass me in my mind and shift. The heat from the flames thrummed in my chest. The Heart of the Sea pulsed alongside my magic, happily content to be in the water. I stretched my wings and long tail like a cat waking from a long nap. Below the surface of the waters, I allowed the fiercest parts of myself to take control and hold the reins for now.

The afternoon sun was so enticing I snapped my wings together and powered myself toward the surface. As I broke into the air, my wings opened in an azure canopy, and I rose above the small beach.

Tiny figures on the sand waved in my direction, but they did not matter to my dragon. I let loose a bright blue stream of flames as I roared across the sky.

Chapter Nine

Zale

I wandered north, beating my wings and lifting myself above the clouds.

Another dragon followed fast behind. It didn't matter. I was free. My dragon bellowed and released another stream of blue flames, unleashing pent-up magic.

In the air or under the sea was where I did my best thinking, and there was much to ponder.

Going to Firestorm may be the best plan, but another way must exist.

A safe cage was still a cage.

I wouldn't live in a cage any longer.

A queen—a High Queen—did not run and hide from danger. Now was the time to stand and fight.

The Shadows needed to be destroyed. Axel and his witch had to be stopped, and who better to do that than me?

At the thought of him, Axel's words came to the front of my mind. *I am not able to sever the cord, but you, dear soulmate, might be able to do it.*

Why was he not able to sever it? He was allegedly full of power. Was this another trap?

Or was he just as willing as I to be free of each other?

Could it be done?

I needed a witch. Thankfully, I knew just who to ask. Good thing we were still in New Orleans. That would save time.

The dragon at my flank roared again, interrupting my thoughts as he spewed green flames across the afternoon sky. I ignored him. Lance would have to keep up if he wanted to come along on my flight.

Several loud pops filled the air and pain sliced through my tail. I roared and twisted my body toward the pain. Below, on the earth's surface, tiny dots scattered on the beach. Flashes exploded around them. I narrowed my dragon's eye and saw the green and brown uniforms scurry. Military.

I tilted my body out to sea, away from their fire. Humans did not recognize friend from foe when it came to the dragons. I smiled in my mind. Perhaps they could be educated? Time would tell. My wings closed tight around my body, and I dipped my head to face the waters below. The air raced around my scales as I plummeted into the sea.

Lance kept pace with me, diving beneath the surface moments behind me. I stretched my tail, and the Heart of the Sea thrummed its approval in my chest. Back and forth, my tail drove me forward. All manner of sea creatures raced to escape my path. The vibrations in the sea spoke their magic to me. I spun so my back was to the sand below. The late afternoon sun cast orange and red beams into the dark waves.

Time lost meaning under the water. There was no war with the Shadows. There were no divisions among the clans. No advisors were plotting my demise. There were no voices in my mind calling me to wander. I could so easily become lost here.

Nothing separated my dragon and me here, and I reveled in our shared connection.

Nyla's face flashed in my mind as the moon rose above the surface.

I nudged my dragon to return, remembering the dragons enslaved to the Shadows. She was reluctant to shift, but it was she who first tried to heal the Shadows after the battle at Las Vegas years ago. She dragged a Shadow dragon into the sea, forcing the ocean to respond. That dragon named us Tiamat. I secretly bound the dragon, Carl, and sent him to be my spy. So, though she was unwilling to yield, my dragon shifted, knowing the importance of this work.

The beach where Nyla waited appeared in the distance, and I pulled my dragon inside my chest. She passed me in my mind, nodding to acknowledge our shared existence before I shifted. As I broke the surface, my lungs filled with air, and I spun to look for Lance.

He followed a moment later, and I glared in his direction as he walked through the waves.

"You were hurt," he accused.

"It was a scratch, healed only a few moments after it happened."

He gripped my shoulders as he reached me. "You were reckless. The humans have killed dragons now. It is not safe to shift, especially in the daylight."

I pushed his hands off and stepped back. "Lance, you do not know me, do you? I do not need your protection. If I'm going to be reckless, I have thought through the consequences."

His face softened and he traced my jaw with his fingers. His words came as a whisper, hardly heard above the surf. "Either way, I will worry. Either way, I will follow."

A flutter in my stomach caused me to think of Axel's words again. I could cut the cord. I laid my palm against Lance's chest. I could give this relationship a chance. I could...rewrite my story. Could I escape the sword above me, waiting to destroy my clan and the rest of dragonkind?

Resolved, I formed a new plan. Cut the cord. Save my clan. Save all of dragonkind. Destroy the Shadows. Live happily ever after.

I slid my hand to Lance's neck and pulled his mouth down to mine. I molded my body to his as his hands slid around my waist and held me close. For the first time, this wasn't goodbye. There was a chance—a chance at happiness. I kissed him with all the hope that rose in my chest.

"Ahem! Excuse me! High Queen, you have some work to do!"

I broke away and felt my cheeks heat. Nyla stood on the beach and waved her arms as she yelled. Three dragons stood behind her. Their Shadows were easily sensed.

"Go." I turned to Lance. "Go. I will call Simeon. Gather the clan to Firestorm. I will meet you there."

His eyes bore into mine before he pulled me close, burying his head in my neck. "Hurry, Zay."

Lance released me and dipped his head. As he stepped away, I snatched his arm and put my lips to his again, only for a moment. My heart thrummed, enjoying this closeness and how easy giving into these feelings became. "I'll see you soon."

He smiled a real smile, one I hadn't seen since our childhood. Is this what happiness was?

As Lance left for the beach, Nyla moved into the waters, the Shadow dragons close behind. Nyla wrapped her arms around me in the waves.

"You are reckless with his heart, Zay. He has always loved you."

I pulled her back and looked her over. Her eyes carried dark circles. Nyla wove an information hub like none other and she was invaluable to me as a spy, but the toll was her constant movement.

"Another time. You need rest, my friend."

Nyla nodded to the three on the beach. "Help them. There are more that come to me every day. Getting them here is what is difficult. And I have no idea how we will get them to Firestorm—"

"That is for me to worry about, Nyla. Now, send them here."

Nyla moved to the beach, where she would remain to protect us as I stripped these dragons of the Shadows. Nyla motioned to me as she spoke to the dragons. With wide eyes, the three waded into the waves. The smallest female reached me first—her face was determined rather than fearful.

Once the other two joined us, I started my magic. Blue smoke from my flames encircled us, shielding the process from those outside.

"Tell me your names."

I learned their names were Ryker, Mara, and the determined one was Eden.

"You understand that in exchange for being stripped of the Shadows, I will bind you in secrecy."

After several mumbled affirmations, I sent flames into the sea. The steam formed old script that hovered in the air as I unraveled the magic of the Shadows. Shadow magic was tricky. It wove its way into a dragon's heart and stitched itself into their souls. The longer the dragon had the Shadows, the deeper the dark magic ran.

I sent more flames into the water's surface and read the old script hovering above. Shadows liked to hide in all sorts of places. Under scales. In vessels. Behind the eyes. The trickiest place to unstitch them was in the chest. Souls were fluid and moving, and the Shadows loved to hide there.

But the sea was also fluid and moving and able to cleanse. The deep magic hummed in my chest as I brought the waters over these dragons, pulling the last of their Shadows from their souls.

When I was done, the look of peace on their faces pierced my heart. It was why I would fight any number of battles, an entire war even, to free dragons from the Shadows. They were free. Free of a cage.

Each time I cleansed a dragon from the Shadows, it strengthened my resolve. I couldn't change my past, but I could free them.

Chapter Ten

Zale

"Can I have your phone? I need to call my brother."

Nyla handed me her phone without question as I stepped out of the waves. "I'll handle them. Go. Call him." She headed off in the direction of the newly freed dragons.

The phone rang three times before he picked up. "Go away."

"No, and if you hang up, I will show up at your island so fast you will think I walked through a portal."

Simeon groaned, and there was rustling through the phone before he finally spoke. "What do you want, Zale?"

"I don't want anything. You need to come here. Now." I stared at the waves and hoped he wouldn't make me go through on my threat to drop everything and hunt him down.

In the silence that followed, I checked the phone to make sure he didn't disconnect me. I softened my tone and tried to reason with him. "Simeon, don't make me force your hand."

"When?"

"Now. The Dragon King...he was here. My advisors will not move to Firestorm without me unless I have protection."

"You don't need my protection."

"No, but they do not know that."

"So tell them. I don't want any part of this war. I have what I need."

My heart fell a little. So much for hoping this would be easy.

"Simeon, I know you saw the golden cord. I...need to do something. Privately."

More silence filled the phone. When Simeon did speak, his voice was low and threatening. "I will not cover for you to see your damned soulmate. He nearly killed mine. He nearly killed me."

"I have no intention of seeing him. I need to see a witch. Marie-Fleur, actually."

He scoffed. "While I fully support anything that will hurt that dragon, do you realize what you are doing? Cutting cords means unraveling a piece of your soul. That kind of damage cannot be undone. That kind of...grief is unfathomable. When Sybil died..." Simeon's silence spoke louder than his words. "Just make sure it is worth it."

"All you need to worry about is getting here. I'll worry about the rest."

"Give us thirty minutes."

"I'll meet you at the Screeching Cauldron."

"Whatever you say." The phone clicked off as Simeon hung up.

His words about the cord hung heavy in my mind. Cutting the cord was the only option, but at what cost? Pain I was familiar with, but so was Simeon. What exactly could be worse?

And why did Axel want me to do this?

The waves reached up to touch my feet, brought close by my unintentional pull for comfort. The ocean swelled around my legs, and then reluctantly retreated back over and over.

"Zay, are you trying to erode the beach? Let the water go."

Nyla waded through the waves to my side as I released my magic. "What did you do with them?"

She placed her hand on her hip and gestured at the dragons walking down the beach. "Ryker and Mara are Mountain clan. I sent them back to their queen. Eden is ours. I'm sending her to the Durban Port in South Africa. She will be able to watch the Shadows there."

"That's close to Firestorm. Has your information indicated they are gathering there?"

Nyla shook her head, her tight curls bouncing around her shoulders. "I want to be prepared. If you are there, he will surely come. That's what you said, right?"

I folded my hands together in front of me and looked out over the sea.

Nyla walked in front of my vision until she met my eyes. "What are you not telling me?"

"It's rather annoying that you are so well-versed in reading me." A smile pulled at my lips.

"I'm a spy. It's what I do."

"I'm glad you are *my* spy then." I hooked my arm in hers and began to walk away from the beach. "What would you have me do to stay safe?"

"I wouldn't have you stay safe. It is not your nature. A moving target is harder to track, but don't change the subject, Zay. What are you keeping from me?"

"I may have a way to be free of this soulmate bond with the Dragon King."

Nyla stopped and pulled me to face her. "May?"

"More than may. I know how to do it. I know who has to do it."

"Then what is stopping you? You know that he tracks you. If it is cut, you are free."

"Axel suggested it."

Nyla looked out over the waves and pondered before looking back at my face, studying my expression. "Even if you do not trust him, this is likely mutually beneficial. I can't see any reason that this is a bad idea."

"Simeon said something—"

"You can't trust that rogue. He speaks only what is helpful to himself."

"He said it is painful to unravel cords. That...it will change me."

Nyla put her hands on my shoulders and looked up into my eyes, a fierce expression on her face. "I don't care how taboo cutting cords is. You are the strongest dragon I know. If there is anyone who can survive this, anyone who deserves the chance to be happy, it is you. Go do this. Be done with that damned king."

I clenched my jaw and nodded. "You're right."

Nyla straightened and rolled her shoulders. "You going to miss me while I'm gone?" She grinned, knowing I would.

"I always do, Nyla. You and Lance are my closest friends. The only ones I truly trust."

"Didn't look like you and Lance were just friends anymore." Nyla's grin broadened into a smile.

"I'm not ready to hope."

"It's a good thing, Zay. He is good for you. Always has been."

My face softened. He was good for me. "How is it that you are always right? Hmm?"

Nyla waded into the waves as purple flames began to spiral around her. "It's my job to know things, my queen. Until next time." She blew me a kiss before diving into the waters. The waves lit up with her shifting. I watched until the dark sea consumed her form.

I walked up the beach, resolved. Now was the time. It was time to find a witch.

Chapter Eleven

Zale

I stood across the street from the Screeching Cauldron with my beignet.

Simeon was late.

Not that I should be surprised by that. He always kept his own timeline.

New Orleans was a strange place. Nothing ever seemed odd or out of place, even after Axel's attack a few months ago. Magic was comfortable here. The entire city thrummed with a vibrant heartbeat.

The little shop had a few visitors in the time I waited. Tourists looking for the local flavor and trinkets. Witches on coven business. No dragons that I could tell, which was good.

I finished my beignet and quietly incinerated the paper that held it.

Where was he?

There was no more point in waiting. Simeon would arrive whenever it suited him. I pushed off the wall I leaned against and headed across the street.

The witch's shop was empty, at least it appeared that way. I let the blue flames from my dragon rise inside of me, heightening my senses.

There was...unusual magic here. It tingled against my skin like a breath of wind or a ripple in the water.

The witch, with her strange blue eyes, appeared before me. Her driftwood skin contrasted sharply with the white dress she wore. She tilted her head, and I lifted my chin as she assessed me.

"I have not had a royal cross my threshold in over a century. What do you want, your highness?"

I raised a brow. I knew who Marie-Fleur was, but we had never met before. "You know who I am?"

"Zale, daughter of Ada and Leo. High Queen of Sea clan."

I relaxed my shoulders a fraction before she continued.

"But that is only the beginning of who you are. Isn't that right?"

My face remained impassive, but my heart rate climbed ever so slightly.

"You wear many faces, High Queen. There are those who know you as Zay. Those who have heard whispers of you as Tiamat. Those who see you as the scorned granddaughter of the former High King. Those who believe you are weak and vulnerable for the chains you bore. Those who believe you are mad and wild for your wandering. And some dragons know you for what you truly are."

I allowed the silence between us for some time before responding. "And who is it that you believe I truly am?"

The witch leaned closer and lowered her voice into a whisper. "A savior."

I pulled my face back a fraction from the witch's intrusion. "I have no idea what you mean."

"You will. In time."

The doorbell behind me jingled, and I swiveled my head to see who approached.

Just inside the door stood Simeon holding his soulmate's hand. His face radiated an expression that was unfamiliar on him. His eyes still glinted with mischief, but he no longer calculated each move I made. His face remained scarred and branded, but almost relaxed. He seemed...whole.

My mind twitched with jealousy. I would never have the kind of peace and joy that comes from a joined soulmate bond. The other half of my soul was determined to enslave our race, destroying it one dragon at a time. And for what purpose? His motives still remained unclear. Bitterness grew around the cord in my heart, and I resented the bond.

"You're late."

He tugged Samara closer and slung his arm around her shoulders as her hazel eyes darted around the shop. "I can always leave if you want."

The witch spoke with her subtle accent. "The ancestors will not allow these two in the cemetery."

I whipped my head back to the witch. "Why would we need to go to the cemetery? And why can they not come?"

Simeon chuckled, and I let out an exasperated breath. "What exactly were you doing these last few months, Simeon?"

He looked at his soulmate and pressed a kiss to her temple. "Why don't you wait outside?"

Samara nodded and darted out of the door with unusual speed.

Simeon crossed his arms over his chest and faced the witch. "Why don't you go ahead and tell her how this all works? I'll stay until she decides how to proceed. You won't have any argument from me if she decides to go to that ancient burial ground. I certainly won't be going back."

It was clear there was more to this story than I realized, but it didn't matter.

"You know why I'm here?" I asked the witch.

"The ancestors are divided on their decision. I have not heard such tremblings and discord from them in many years. You are here about your soulmate cord, are you not?"

I nodded. "I want it severed."

Marie-Fleur moved quickly about the shop, gathering various items and tucking them into a satchel at her side. "Then hurry. We need to go quickly."

"What does speed have to do with this?"

Marie-Fleur was in my face once again. "The Dragon King grows stronger by the hour. I will have to bind him in the circle to sever the cord."

"You have the strength to bind the Dragon King?"

"Only for a short time. That's why we must hurry."

The witch pushed past us and bustled out of the shop. I moved to follow her, but Simeon stepped in my way. He grabbed my arm and I snapped my face to his, blue fire flooding my vision.

His own eyes flashed with white flames. "Are you certain, Zale? The Dragon King doesn't bargain with anyone. He always has a plan. There must be a reason he wants you to do this, and it can't be good."

"Would you want to be tied to a monster? Doomed to never join with your soulmate?"

Simeon dropped his hand. His mouth parted as if he were about to speak, but then he clamped it closed.

"That's what I thought."

I made it to the shop door before he spoke again.

"I'll be waiting for you, Zale, when it's all over. I hope you know what you are doing."

I glanced at him over my shoulder for a moment before leaving the shop and following the witch to the cemetery.

Chapter Twelve

Zale

I crossed the threshold of the cemetery, past the stone ladies, and my magic pulled on me like a stretched rubber band. The sea called and asked me to return, but I pushed forward, my mind resolved.

Marie-Fleur stopped in front of a tomb, cracked down the center as if the occupant had burst forth from inside. Her white dress swished in the wind, and she turned to face me.

"Why do you want this?"

"My reasons are my own."

She closed her eyes and hummed softly. "The ancestors are divided. Your own ancestors push and pull over whether to grant this."

I bristled at her words. "No one gets to decide my destiny but me. My past does not define me. My choices now do."

The witch's lips quirked slightly. "I agree with you. We will see if the ancestors will grant their cooperation. A soulmate bond is not an easy thing to unravel."

"Unravel? Won't you cut it?"

A laugh emitted from the witch. "Have you ever seen the cords? The one that ties you to the Dragon King?"

She wanted to shame me, but I refused to allow her that hold over my emotions. "You know I have not."

Marie-Fleur pulled a length of rope from her pouch and pulled it taught between her hands. "Do you see how the strands wrap together and each strand strengthens the rope?"

I nodded, and she continued.

"The soulmate cord is thicker than any other bond. It has many strands, all connected to your soul. I will cut each one until the cord unravels."

"Explain. How is this done?"

The witch pulled more items from the satchel at her hip. "First, we will create a circle of salt, focusing the earth's power in one place. Then we will summon your soulmate here."

"Here?"

"Here. If the ancestors are favorable, they will hold him here until we are done."

"He is the one who suggested this. You think he will not agree?"

The witch chuckled as she began to spread the salt in a circle. "He is foolish. He believes this will set him free."

"What happens when he is in the circle?"

"Both of your powers will be void during the process. You will both be immobilized so you are not harmed any further."

Any further? "Will he be able to see me? Talk to me?"

"Of course." The witch completed the circle of salt and then stepped inside. "Are you ready?"

I thought of all my clan and the dragons enslaved to the Shadows. They needed a leader who was not divided because of a soulmate bond. No matter the pain, my empire needed a chance to overcome this evil. "Yes. Do it."

"As you wish, High Queen."

And then I thought of myself and of the chains I bore before. This should feel like ridding myself of them. So why did a thread of fear weave its way into my mind? In my heart?

I shook away the feeling and focused on the witch. She began to chant in a language I did not know. The sea often granted me understanding, but my familiar magic was far from me now.

I bit down on the inside of my cheek. This was right. Right?

Shadows formed before me and merged into a shape I knew well. Axel's gray eyes bore into me, anger swirling in their depths. He looked around at the cemetery and the witch before looking back into my eyes—a smirk formed on his face.

"So you decided to do it."

"Don't act surprised. This is what is best."

He lifted one brow. "You'll have no argument from me. Joining with me or destroying this bond, either way, it doesn't matter to me."

I narrowed my eyes. "What makes you think I would join with you?"

He laughed, but there was little humor there. "I'm your soulmate, princess. Not even your cold heart could resist that bond."

"Well, we won't have to find out now, will we?"

The witch's words grew louder and fire flamed around the edges of the circle she had created. Smoke filled the space between us and something golden glinted in the light. I focused on it, only to realize it was a thick golden cord stretched tight between my chest and Axel's. I looked down at my chest, and cords stretched out in all directions. Each one varied in thickness and color.

I gently lifted my hand and touched the cords extending from my body. How could I never know this magic was here when it was so clearly a part of me? My fingers found the gold one. It was thicker, with more strands than any of the others. I ran my fingers along the edge and Axel visibly shivered. I looked up at his face as my hand touched the cord.

A strange look crossed his face. No cords rose up from his chest except the gold one between us. His chest looked strangely bare compared to mine. As I traced my fingers along the cord, I examined his face again. It was...pained? Peaceful?

I hardly knew him. It was hard to tell.

"Have you never seen them before?" Axel opened his eyes and grumbled in my direction.

"No. I'm not rogue."

"You've never felt the touch of someone on the other end of your cord?"

Then Axel grinned and lifted his hand. He brought it down heavily on the cord and gripped it tightly.

I gasped as all the breath escaped out of my lungs. Ice gripped my chest, and I shuddered, struggling to pull in more air. I stared at Axel, willing him to release me, but his smile widened.

"Doesn't feel good, does it, princess?"

He released the cord and ran his fingers gently along the edges. I sucked in a breath as his grip broke. Heat flooded me as his fingers grazed the edges of our cord. Warmth and pleasure rose inside me as he continued.

"Stop."

"Why? You'll never feel it again. Don't you want to know what it is like to have a soulmate?"

"No. Not one like you."

"What? Not like what?"

"A leviathan."

The look on his face told me my words stuck. "What did you call me?"

"A leviathan. That's what I call any dragon who would willingly enslave his entire race."

I glared at Axel, and he returned my gaze, flames rising in his eyes. The witch stood between us, her knife poised over the cord. She lowered it toward the soulmate bond. Before the knife touched, a fourth person appeared in the circle and held the witch's wrist.

I faced the new arrival. Her blue eyes bore into mine as they had many times when she was alive.

"Keani?"

"Stop this foolishness. At once."

Chapter Thirteen

Zale

"What do you mean stop?" I yelled at my aunt. "How are you even here?"

Her blue eyes were ice as they bore into mine. "Doing this will change the future."

"I'm aware. It's why I'm doing it."

Keani's eyes flashed with flames. "It changes not just your story. It changes the whole story."

"It doesn't matter. I need to do this. I need to be set free. For our clan. For those that are enslaved."

Flames spiraled around Keani as her voice rose and the ground trembled with her words. "Foolish girl! You understand nothing! See it for yourself."

I hardly had time to wrinkle my brows at her confusing words when blue smoke swirled around us. I glanced at Axel, and he watched with intrigue as the smoke swirled around us until he and I appeared alone.

He glanced around, noticing the golden rays of sun glint off the waters beyond the balcony. "What is this magic?"

"It's sea magic. A vision."

"Where are we?"

I looked around and noticed the carvings on the wall behind me and the angle of the coast beyond the balcony. "It looks like Firestorm."

"A sea province," he murmured. "What are we doing here?"

"I doubt we are here. This feels like a vision, not reality."

He walked to the balcony, finally able to move. "What purpose does this dragon have for showing us?"

Before I could answer, the door behind us moved open. A couple laughed as they careened into the room. They shut the door quickly behind them and locked in an embrace, completely oblivious to us standing in the room. I was startled when I realized it was me—a vision of me...and Axel.

I watched as he gently ran his hand down her face before tugging her to him and locking his lips with hers. He was different. The shape of his jaw and the glint in his eyes were the same, but he was also something more. The vision of myself clung to his shirt, and I watched as he backed her toward a bed in the room.

"Keani, this isn't funny. Stop this!"

The couple continued past me and collapsed onto the bed. Warmth flooded my body, and I felt the vision as if it were happening actively to me. My heart thrummed happily despite my growing discomfort.

"Enough." I waved my arm and dissolved the magic in the room.

Suddenly, the fog thickened and closed in around us once more. The scene shifted, and we stood on the cliffs I frequently wandered near the Arctic Circle. A vision of Axel and myself sat and leaned against each other, their legs dangling over the edge.

Axel walked up next to me, and we watched the vision versions of ourselves.

The vision Axel tilted his head toward the vision of me. "Do you think we can save them?"

"The Shadow dragons?"

"Yes. Do you think we can find them and save them?"

The vision version of myself reached out and grasped his hand. "Together. We will find them and save them. Together."

My heart twisted. This wasn't what I wanted to see. I wanted to be free of this soulmate bond. I didn't want to see how it could be. That didn't mean it would be that way.

Right?

Doubt crept into my mind. I glanced over at Axel, envisioning him in a new light. Could the other half of my soul be as dreadful as I built him up in my mind? Maybe there was a path where we made each other better? Maybe there was a way I could have it all.

Then the reality of our world came crashing over me like a tidal wave.

Axel created the Shadows.

Axel used them to enslave our race.

Axel killed my family line. My grandfather, father, and mother.

And he would not stop.

Keani's visions were cruel.

"Stop this, Keani!" I screamed at the night sky. Silence cut through the vision with clarity but did not dissolve it.

"What do you think the point of all this is?" Axel asked.

I crossed my arms and stared into his eyes. "To make me change my mind. To do whatever the ancestors are bidding me to do."

Axel lifted his hand toward my face, and I watched it like the threat it was.

"Do you think..."

He raised his hand, and with the lightest touch, he set my skin burning as he grazed his fingertips down my jaw.

"Do you think there was ever a chance for the two of us?"

My heart raced in my chest as fear, hope, and uneasiness collided together inside me like waves tossed in the sea.

I lifted my hand and pressed it against his, holding his hand to my face. My magic thrummed happily inside me. It was almost peaceful to have his skin against mine, even in the slightest.

My eyes closed. It hurt to be so close to my soulmate, knowing he would never be able to be what I needed. He would never change.

I would never be whole.

I opened my eyes and released his hand. "No. There was never a chance."

Axel's gray eyes never left mine as his face settled into stone. He tugged on the cuff of his shirt and righted himself.

"Keani! End this!"

The fog vanished, and I stood in the salt circle. My soulmate before me. The witch and my aunt between us.

Keani stepped toward me, leaning close enough for only my ears to hear. "You will regret this, Zale." As quickly as she had appeared moments earlier, she was gone—a fine mist left in her wake.

The golden tether shone vibrantly in the cemetery. Marie-Fleur raised her knife and brought it down, hovering over the cord.

Axel locked his eyes with mine, his mouth set in a grim line.

"Shall I proceed?" The witch's voice seemed far away as she asked, or maybe the beating of my heart in my ears muffled the sound.

"Yes. I want this done."

Marie-Fleur began to chant once again as she brought the knife down on the cord. Magic flashed from both Axel and me as the first strand separated.

Deep pain flickered to life in my chest. I willed my lungs to breathe through it and grit my teeth.

She sawed with her knife through more strands of the cord.

Each strand severed burned and lay limp. The gold changed to morose ash as the strands...died.

It was alive. The cord. Our magic. Separate from us but holding us connected at the same time.

More visions flashed in my mind, and I raised a clenched fist to my forehead at the pain. Axel's lips on my skin. Axel's magic pulsing in my veins. Axel's hand in mine as we faced the Shadows.

Tears streamed down my cheeks as the pain overwhelmed my senses. I could no longer power my mind over the stabbing ache in my chest.

I wanted to tell her to stop. I wanted to take it back. I wanted to keep this part of myself alive, but I couldn't move. I couldn't breathe.

There was no way to know how long this continued. I was powerless to stop it, and it wrecked me.

Ages passed in my mind's eye. My magic tried to compensate for the part of me that was dying by sending flames spiraling around and flashing erratically from inside me.

I don't know how, but when Marie-Fleur reached the final strand of that golden cord, I knew. My eyes snapped open, and I watched Axel as we died. His white flames were spiraling around him, and there was a pop as the final strand severed.

Magic lashed between us. My blue flames struck him as his white ones marked me, both thrust out of the circle.

I collapsed on my back and stared at the stars above me. Somehow, I knew they had moved. Nothing was the same.

This was a new world.

One where I no longer had a soulmate.

Chapter Fourteen

Zale

Tears streamed down my temples as I lay there and stared at the night sky.

My dragon roared and moaned inside of me, consuming all the thoughts inside my mind. All I heard was her pain.

Is this what it was like to break?

My magic pulsed around me, and blue flames licked around my vision, sputtering and flaring to life irregularly. My dragon thrashed against the mind wall, begging to shift, but I didn't know how. I didn't know...anything.

Closing my eyes, I floated in a free fall. I pushed back against my dragon and her sounds faded to silence. A ringing filled my ears and I winced against the pain.

Get up.

My fingers twitched at the command.

Get up, High Queen.

The voice. It was not my own, even though it echoed on the walls of my mind.

I sat up and sucked in a breath, my lungs aching as they worked. Everything...hurt.

I groaned and gripped my chest. The pain expanded and rushed through my veins with each heartbeat. It threatened to pull me back into the black abyss.

"Get up."

My head snapped to the voice.

Keani stood before me, her blue flames and water wrapped around her body. Her eyes were filled with anger I did not know she possessed. She crossed her arms over her chest and looked my body over once again before repeating her command. "Get up."

I grit my teeth and pushed myself to my feet. The scent of smoke and blood surrounded me. My vision tunneled on my aunt, and I stumbled. I willed each muscle to listen to my commands and stand me straight.

As I righted myself, she put her hands on my shoulders. "High Queen, I will not be able to help you further. The ancestors are...unhappy. You have altered the course of history one too many times and they will not be so forgiving on your future. So I will leave you with this piece of advice. When you are ready, when you are in need, when you have recovered what is lost, and everything is dark, follow the voice."

The ache deep inside of me fogged my mind, and I wanted to hear her repeat it so I wouldn't forget. "What are you saying, Keani?"

"That is all I can tell you." She leaned forward and kissed my forehead. "Go."

Like vapors of steam, she drifted away in the night. In her absence, the pulse of my pain threatened to send me back to the ground. An image of myself in front of a mirror and a crown on my head flashed in my mind.

I couldn't lie down and die. I was queen. A High Queen.

Of what?

I tried to follow the thread of thought in my mind, but it escaped my grasp. I pressed the heel of my hand against my eyes. When the wave of pain eased, I dropped my hands and looked around.

Tombs of cement rose all around me. Salt scattered around the ground—some in a circle, and some appeared as if it was blown about by a strong wind.

Two forms lay just beyond the salt, neither moving. I walked with heavy steps to the first one. Her white dress was covered in soot and torn in odd places. Maroon blood pooled beneath her and stained her clothes. Her odd blue eyes stared openly at the night sky, and her slack jaw gaped open.

I knew this dead woman. What was she to me?

Witch.

I chased down that thought, but it escaped me like the last. Her name eluded me as well.

I looked at the other form. He lay on his side, his back to me, but I knew him.

How?

Who was he?

When I reached his body, I gripped his shoulder and turned him on his back. He groaned but did not open his eyes.

A gasp escaped me when the memories flooded back to me.

Axel.

The cord.

All the visions.

Every minute of our history together.

Tears followed the pain that washed through me. I reached out to touch his face again. Shadows swelled around him, and I snatched my hand back away from the dark magic, fearing it would take me too. As he disappeared into the darkness, I thought I would feel sad or full of regret, but it was so much worse.

I was *empty*.

He was nothing to me. I was nothing to him. It was complex. I cared deeply for him and had not known it before. He was part of me. I was a part of him. And now...we were nothing.

And I felt nothing.

Nothing except the pain that wanted to sweep through me like a cold raging sea—unforgiving and without mercy.

A sense of urgency filled me, and I knew I needed to be somewhere. I paced the ground, trying to remember.

Where was I supposed to be?

I wasn't exactly sure.

My mind swirled between my dragon retreating and the pain. I struggled to catch my thoughts. I walked through the raised tombs until I stood between two stone ladies at the gate.

I looked to the left and right, unsure of which way to turn.

Wander.

I shook my head. The voice that haunted me seemed familiar. What else did I have to do?

Wander seemed as good a task as any.

The way to the right led to the ocean. I was sure, even though I did not remember why I knew. I took off at a sprint to the right. The sea would know what to do. I ignored the doubt that wanted control of my thoughts. Water would restore me.

It had to.

Chapter Fifteen

Zale

My legs burned, but I pushed this frail form further, sprinting faster.

Water.

I needed it.

I needed it more than the next breath.

"Zale!"

The voice was familiar, but the name was a tendril of smoke I couldn't quite grasp. I kept going.

The sea called to my heart, pulling me in like a riptide.

When I turned the corner and the water spread before me, I paused. A woman stood directly in my path, her hand on her hip and her head delicately tilted to the side. Her lips twisted back as she grinned like a predator with her prey.

I was not her prey.

I was no one's prey.

I was the dangerous one. That much I knew.

She flipped her honey-blond hair over her shoulder, and dark Shadows began to weave around her, dancing and spiraling around her like smoke. A chain of gold appeared in her free hand from the Shadows.

"Looking for water, High Queen?"

My face wanted to twitch, but I knew not to reveal anything. Stone cold and frozen, I kept my face void of expression as I fought to remember who this was. I should have known her.

"I'm afraid he's running a bit late, but I'll be sure to keep you company while we wait. You have something I need." Her voice purred with the taunt.

Who was *he*?

What did they need?

White and orange flames flashed at my side, and a stream shot directly toward the woman before me. She lifted the Shadows and they formed a shield that easily deflected the fire. I snapped my head to my side and a dark-haired girl stood a few feet away. Her hazel eyes flashed with deadly flames. She didn't even acknowledge my presence, but since she could have sent those flames into me and did not, I assumed she was a friend.

The first woman lowered her shield and it dissipated in the wind. "Samara. Did you think I had not prepared? Where is your soulmate? I wasn't quite finished with him, and I would love another...taste."

The woman beside me—Samara—clenched her fist and fire spiraled down her arm. "Around."

"Pity. I guess we can play our old games instead."

I flinched as a hand touched my elbow. How had I missed someone approaching? My head whipped to the side, and pale green eyes glared back at me. I knew him. He was important to me.

Simeon.

"What the hell were you doing, Zale? Wait. Don't bother answering that. Just get to the water. We will handle the Dragon King's witch."

I blinked as my mind assaulted me with memories of the two of us as children. We ran and played. We attended lessons from Keani and Ada. We hid in the library at Firestorm after frustrating our teachers.

The memories broke as Simeon stepped in front of me. "Do you know me?"

I nodded.

He stared at me before moving to Samara's side. He called over his shoulder, "Get to the water."

The two of them circled the witch and began mercilessly firing flames at her. She deflected each one but did not return their fire. Her eyes darted to me.

A wave crashed on the bank and called to my fractured soul, begging me to come closer, reaching for me.

I made it three steps before a wind threw me back onto the grassy bank..

My head knocked against the rocks and grass. Stars burst in my vision. Blue flames flickered around my body but didn't reach my head. Pieces of hair plastered to my face, and I swept it aside as I pushed myself to sitting.

A black dragon larger than any I had ever seen before loomed before me. The only dragon that large was...

The Dragon King.

Axel.

Memories rushed through my mind. I moved to a crouch as I began to put the pieces together and push the fog away. My soulmate was before me. He and I were—had been connected.

His wings spread in a smoky canopy and his head weaved back and forth on his serpentine neck. Overlapping obsidian scales covered his body. At his chest, red flames gathered. No, wait. Those weren't flames. They were...scars. As he called his white flames forward, the angry red marks seemed to glow. A furious look flashed in his eyes, and I knew he would kill me.

I rolled to the side out of the path of the flames as he opened his mouth and released his fire.

I beat against the wall in my mind that my dragon had built between us. When she wouldn't respond to me, I called on our magic, but that didn't work either. I couldn't call for smoke to hide me. I couldn't call for flames to protect me or heal me.

Vulnerability makes some quake in fear.

I didn't have that luxury.

Instead, the danger began to clear my mind of the cobwebs.

My clan depended on me.

Dragons needed my help.

I severed my cord in two so I could do what needed to be done.

The fact that my dragon ignored me would have to wait.

Rising to my feet as I gripped earth in my fist, I stared at the Dragon King. All I needed was to get to the water. It would fill the void in my soul. It would tear down the wall my dragon built between us. It would heal me.

When the black dragon lowered his head to snap at me, I hurled the dirt at his eye. Unfortunately, it wouldn't hurt him, but maybe it would buy me a moment. He roared as I sprinted directly toward the creature's legs and the water he stood in. Almost there.

A taloned claw gripped my chest and crushed my body to the ground.

The pressure cracked my sternum, and all the air left my lungs. I wanted to scream, but that would require pulling in another breath. I gripped the claw and twisted, trying to move it, but the dragon held me steady. He tilted his face and opened his jaws. Fire erupted from him, and I knew that was the end. I stared directly at the beast. I would meet death head-on, not cower in fear. That would be giving him more power than he had.

Deep blue light from inside my chest rose up and encased me. It was so deep that the light was almost black—almost an absence of light. It was different from my flames but still familiar.

The Heart of the Sea.

The strange magic lifted around me and pushed back the black dragon's flames. With one pulse, it sent Axel and everyone else spiraling away from me. Axel shifted as he tumbled to the grass, leaving the still form of a man on the edge of the water.

I moved my head, and darkness clouded the edges of my vision. Pain unmeasurable still pulsed in my body. The cracked bones hurt too. I lifted my hand toward the water, calling it to me. The water flowed easily to my hand and covered my body. My mind began to slip into the abyss, and panic threatened to close my throat when the water did not heal me.

It should have eased my suffering.

It should have made everything better.

So why did I still ache as badly as I did standing in that cemetery?

With my senses beginning to dull, I embraced the abyss. Maybe healing could be found there instead.

Chapter Sixteen

Zale

I inhaled sharply as fingers traced down my face.

My eyes opened wide.

I knew the canopy above me, but I couldn't remember the name. "Zay?"

Sitting up, I scanned the room. The deep blues and golden accents told me I was in a Sea clan castle, but how was I here? The last thing I remembered was being on the beach.

A man with umber skin and eyes as dark as night sat on the side of the bed. His face seemed familiar, and his presence did something to my mind. I struggled to pull his name or who he was to me. Was he a friend? Was he the enemy?

I called my dragon to the surface, preparing to protect myself. I met resistance, my magic blocked by her defiance. What...what...was happening?

"Zay? It's Lance. Don't you know me?"

His face was new in my mind. It was familiar, but it was...new. Everything had shifted.

"I need a blade."

His face scrunched in confusion. What was he doing sitting on the side of my bed? Images of his hands on me, his lips on mine, flashed in my mind.

"A blade?"

I heard a noise outside the room, and I turned toward it. Where was my dragon? Why would she not respond to me?

"Zale, what do you remember?"

There should be a blade in this room—my room. I knew this room, but it wasn't home. Somehow, I knew I had no home now. The desk had blades, and so did the largest book on the bookcase. The headboard! I twisted around and found the release on the headboard. A blade tumbled into my hand, and I wrapped my hand around it like a lifeline.

Lance stood from the bed and raised his hands in the air. "High Queen, I am not a threat. What is going on?"

High Queen.

Of Sea clan.

That's who I was.

Like a tidal wave, the memories flooded my mind again. The cord. Axel—the Dragon King. The witch and the cemetery. And the beach, where the ocean healed me. Did it heal me?

I looked down at my chest. No bruises. I had no pain when I moved.

My human form was healed, but my dragon retreated further away every time I called to her in my mind.

Not only was I the High Queen of a ruthless clan, I was now vulnerable.

I rose to my feet, my head swimming with the movement, but I remained upright.

Lance watched me with wary eyes, and I moved past him to the balcony.

Firestorm.

That's where I was—our clan's most secure and secluded sanctuary. Here, we could hide or withstand a siege for many years. I gripped the railing and looked out over the ocean. The waves mocked me and my withdrawn dragon. I clenched my teeth and begged my dragon to come to me, but she resisted still.

The door to my room opened, and I turned to see Simeon standing in the entrance. I marched to him, and he closed the door behind himself.

"What happened?"

"I told you it was a bad idea." He raised a brow and I wanted to hurt him.

I drew the blade from its sheath and pressed the tip to his throat. "I don't want to play any games. What. Happened?"

Simeon smirked despite the pressure I held against his neck. "That's interesting. If I were you, High Queen, I wouldn't let on that you can't use your magic."

I dropped the blade and sent it tip over hilt into the eye of a portrait on the wall.

"With or without my magic, I am still High Queen. I am also still deadly. If you want a conversation, go find your soulmate. I'm in no mood for battle of wills."

Simeon grinned. "The witch cut the cord. You no longer have a soulmate."

"I'm aware. What happened after that?"

"Your ex-soulmate, former soulmate? What do we call it? There should be a name for it—"

"Enough!"

"The Dragon King used your weakness when the cord was cut to try and kill you."

"How did he know I would be weak?"

"My guess? It wasn't the first time he had a cord cut. Actually, that makes a lot of sense. I've never come across him, and I track every cord I see."

He didn't have other cords. I remembered that from the cemetery. "How did I get here? What happened to him?"

"Samara and I brought you here—You're welcome. We went back to see what happened to them, but they were already gone."

Another knock sounded at the door, but I ignored it.

"Is that all?"

"I expected a thank you."

"You won't get it, Simeon. You swore your loyalty to Sea clan. It is what I expect of you."

The knock sounded at the door again. He grinned. "Looks like I arrived just in time for all the fun. See you out there."

Simeon pulled the door open, and a surprised advisor jumped out of his way as he exited the room. Lance walked to my side and placed his hand on my shoulder. He would have to stay close. I truly was vulnerable for the first time.

"Your Highness, the families are waiting for you to address them. It is considered rude not to greet them as they arrive, and you've already avoided them—"

"I have avoided no one." I clasped my hands in front of me. "I have been otherwise engaged. I'll see them now."

"Very good. I'll let them know."

Lance leaned down after the dragon left and whispered, "Zay, are you sure you're ready?"

I pulled myself from his touch. Something didn't feel quite right about it now.

"I am their High Queen. It does not matter if I am ready."

Chapter Seventeen

Zale

I followed the advisor down the hall of the ancient fortress with Lance at my side. My mind darted through everything I could remember, and I wondered how I would manage whatever awaited me.

My dragon continued to ignore me. Ironic that she chose a cage in my mind when I had worked so hard to free us from them.

My fingers traced the place on my chest where the stone resided, and my heart began to race.

He would come for me.

Axel wouldn't rest until he had the Heart of the Sea.

He tried to kill me. When he came to try again, would I be able to protect myself?

I blinked away those thoughts as we reached the doors that opened to the throne room. The advisor pushed open the wooden doors, and the voices hushed as I stepped forward.

Firestorm was the first place Sea clan laid down roots after the binding.

Patterns of browns and golds and blues scattered the raised ceilings. The sand-colored walls were interrupted with floor-to-ceiling windows. Curtains blew gently in the hot breeze, and columns of blue and white alternated a path to the throne.

My throne.

I clasped my hands before myself and scanned the dragons as I walked the aisle. Each of them assessed me with calculated envy. Power in Sea clan was our currency.

And now, I was as good as penniless.

I held my head high until I reached the throne. Turning with purpose, I scanned the dragons before me. There were very few that my mind recalled. I reached out to my dragon again, and she retreated. I was on my own.

Sitting on the throne, I placed my hands on the arms and waited for the dragons to resume their conversations.

"Your Highness."

I met the gaze of a dragon with sea-green eyes. He was important, but his name escaped me. I nodded for him to continue.

"High Queen, the Shadows have been attacking major cities worldwide. Many are close to Sea clan settlements. Our information tells us the Dragon King is looking for..."

"For what? What does your information say?"

The dragon's eyes darted around the room, and he stepped closer to the throne. "For you, highness."

Carl. That was his name. The first Shadow dragon I turned. An information source on the eastern coast of the United States. This was not his usual appearance. He had cleaned himself up for this meeting.

He was a friend.

I gave him a small smile. "You're right. He is looking for me. What would you advise me to do?"

Carl dipped his head. "That is not for me to say, my queen."

"I'm asking. What would you advise?"

He lifted his eyes, and the wrinkles at the corners betrayed the depth of his age. "Wander, my queen."

My face became stone and I locked my breath in my chest.

Wander. Like the voice told me. Did Carl know this voice? Was it a coincidence that he used that word?

Lance stepped closer to my side, and his voice dripped with formality as he spoke to Carl. "Is that all?"

The dragon nodded and retreated from the throne. I watched him weave his way out of the throne room, my eyes tracking his every movement. What did he know? I should follow—

Several advisors approached me at once. "High Queen. We would like to present you with our plan of attack."

I tilted my head to assess them. Each of them held the hardened expressions of Sea clan. I raised a brow. "There will not be any attacks. Send word to our scouts and spies. I want every Sea dragon called back to Firestorm."

The advisors glanced at each other. "But Your Highness—"

"Now. I want you to call everyone back and prepare for a siege."

One advisor stepped forward, and she widened her stance as she spoke. "Sea clan does not back down from a war, Your Majesty."

"We are not retreating. We are planning." I stood and addressed each of the advisors before me. "Prepare for a battle, but it will be here—at Firestorm."

"There hasn't been a battle at Firestorm in centuries."

"Then you had better get to work."

I relaxed my stance and slowly moved past them, Lance on my heels.

"Your Majesty, the Mountain clan. We have questions about their arrival."

My feet stopped. Without turning, I looked over my shoulder and spoke from my chest. "Our Mountain cousins are welcome here at

Firestorm. Anyone who says differently will answer directly to me. On penalty of exile or death, they are not to be harmed."

The Heart of the Sea thrummed in my chest, embedding my words with power—a direct order from the source of our magic.

So I wasn't defenseless. I wasn't completely alone, but would the sea respond to my will, or would I be subject to it?

I set my face toward the door and moved with purpose to escape these dragons. Lance continued as my shadow. He took my elbow when we entered the hallways and pulled me to a side room.

"Zay, what was that? I thought your dragon was..."

"The Heart of the Sea. It spoke through me." Silence swelled between us at the gravity of how magic was changing. "Lance, I need you to do something for me."

He took my hand and brought it to his lips, pressing a soft kiss to my palm. "Anything for you."

"Nyla. Can you get her back here? Use any means you can to reach her. I need the people I trust most if I'm to face the Shadows in battle."

He dropped my hand and nodded. "I'll send for her."

My eyes lifted to his. "When will Mountain clan be here?"

"The Mountain Queen sent word that they will be arriving the day after tomorrow. The portal dragons have already arrived." He paused, and concern spread over his face. "Do you think you will be able to control the infighting?"

"You assume that there will be fighting."

"You are foolish if you think there won't be."

I walked around him and placed my hand on the door to the room, pausing to look back at him as I spoke. "There is a Shadow army with the Dragon King ready to break down our walls. There will be plenty of fighting for everyone."

Chapter Eighteen

Zale

I waited outside the portal for my cousin. She should have arrived by now. I shifted my weight and glanced around at the windows where the light streamed in.

"Do you think she is detained?"

"Jenna will be here." Simeon stood at my side, awaiting the Mountain clan's arrival.

"She said she would come at noon. What do you think is going on?"

Simeon nudged me with his shoulder. "Zale, she's fine."

"The Shadows control the Heart of the Mountain. We don't know how that will affect their magic."

Samara stood silently at Simeon's side. She rarely spoke in the last few days since I awoke. Perhaps that was how she always was. I hardly knew my brother's soulmate. Other than her battle to free herself from the Shadows, I knew little else.

At least she fought to be free. The same couldn't be said of my former soulmate.

Finally, the light on the portal began to shimmer. The edges of the mirror lit up in old script, the words binding the magic together and letting the surface ripple like something thrown into still waters.

The lights flickered and then went out. That shouldn't have happened.

Samara stepped toward the mirror and traced the writing. "Something's wrong."

"Samara..." Simeon stepped forward.

The lights along the mirrored edge flared to life.

"Samara." Simeon reached forward and pulled her back, his voice pinched with concern.

Shadows slithered along the edges of the portal. My stomach clenched. I knew that something was wrong.

Sounds of fighting and yelling sounded in the room, emitting from the portal. My mind snapped into place and I knew what needed to happen.

"Simeon. I don't have access to my dragon. Go. Hold off the Shadows."

He nodded once, his white and orange flames spiraling down his arm. Samara took his hand and led the way through the portal.

With hurried steps, I opened the door to the guards standing outside. "Sound the alarms. The Shadows are here."

One dragon took off down the hall, and the other took his place at my side. I wished for Lance, knowing he would have my back no matter the enemy. The sooner he brought Nyla back, the better. I needed my allies close.

My guard's green flames waited along his arms and chest, prepared to strike. I sorted through our resources with one-half of my mind while the other half worried over myself.

Would Axel come for me?

Would the Heart of the Sea hold him off?

Would my dragon care?

Would she answer me?

Then, the most horrible thought crossed my mind. *What if I lost my clan? What if I failed?*

Shadows snaked around the shimmering mirror. They grew larger only to be made small again. I shook away the thoughts for myself and focused on the problem before me.

Three forms poured out of the mirror's surface.

Samara's eyes glowed white and orange with her flames. She pushed the two toward me. "Take them. Get them out of here!"

She turned and melted back into the portal, leaving Jesse and Maddie stumbling in front of me. Jesse wrapped his arm around Maddie's waist and pulled her to himself. His eyes met mine. This Knight was one of the bravest humans I ever had the pleasure of meeting. This time, Jesse's face dripped with fear.

"Zale."

The guard at my side growled his dissent. "That is not how you address our High Queen."

Ignoring the formalities that my role demanded, I guided them toward the door. "Take them to my chambers, Kai. Stay with them."

"No!" Jesse glared at my guard. "No dragons."

Maddie's arms wrapped around her abdomen. Her enlarged abdomen.

He fears for his child.

"Jesse. What's happening on the other side?"

He reached behind his back, pulled a gun, released the safety, and held it at his side. "Shadows. Take us somewhere secure. I will handle our safety."

The portal began to light up again. "Kai, get them to my chambers and then return here. Now."

My guard dipped his chin before rushing the humans out of the portal room. I spun and faced the mirror. My own reflection projected on the surface. I saw my fear. I saw my doubt.

I adjusted the weaknesses, replacing them with a fire that could only come from my humanity. It was the first time in my life that I was thankful for the time I had hidden my true nature. I found strength from all aspects of my being. And right now? My clan needed me. The Heart of the Sea rested inside me. Whatever came through that mirror, I would face it.

Even if it were the Dragon King himself.

I called to my dragon, hoping against hope that maybe she would choose that moment, when I was in danger, to respond.

Silence.

I was alone.

Ripples across the surface drew me back to the present. The writing flared bright along the portal.

Samara rushed through again. This time, with younglings. I pointed them in the direction of the door.

"Here. This way."

Come on, Sea clan. Where are you?

After the younglings came more of the Mountain clan through the portal. Dragon after dragon emerged with evidence of the battle on the other side of the portal—burns, soot, blood.

I scanned the faces for those who were mine—Simeon, Jenna. Where were they?

Finally, my clan began to arrive, pouring into the room where Mountain clan dragons emerged. I shouted my orders over the chaos, directing my warriors inside the room and my advisors to take the Mountain clan to safety. The dragons became fewer and fewer through the portal. I kept expecting Shadows to appear, but nothing.

The mirror with its gold inscriptions remained lit, and I waited, my warriors at my side.

Still my cousin did not emerge.

Still Simeon remained on the other side of the portal with his soulmate.

Chapter Nineteen

Zale

I t was almost anticlimactic to wait on the other side of the portal, wondering who or what would emerge on the other side.

The portal became brighter than ever before, and I shielded my eyes.

What was happening?

The mirror reflected the brightness of flames colliding and, when it dimmed, the Dragon King's witch stepped through the portal. She played with the Shadows as they danced around her in an ethereal pattern.

"Hello, Sea clan."

I curled my lip and clasped my hands together in front of my waist. "Kill her," I ordered.

Celeste lifted a brow in my direction and gracefully met my clan's attack. She danced with the dark magic, sending my clanmates spiraling away with each blow. More Shadow dragons poured from the portal, entering my sanctuary.

With the stone in my chest, I reached out to the sea, asking her to destroy the witch. The ocean didn't respond. I begged the magic to be released and save my clan. It remained cold and silent. How could it abandon me now?

My guards stayed at my sides, fighting off each advance of the Shadows to reach me.

Where were they? Jenna? Simeon?

We needed to close the portal. *Now.* Before any more Shadow dragons poured in.

I swallowed down the screams inside myself, begging them to wait a little longer.

"Take down the portal," I ordered, motioning to the mirror. The guards moved from my sides, and I melted back into my clan, watching the battle. Shadow dragons fell as often as the Sea warriors did, but their numbers were replaced with more cursed dragons pouring out of the portal.

My guards sent fire into the portal as they reached it, and the edges singed and hissed.

It would take more than a few dragons to take down this portal. I called to my dragon within me, and she refused me.

Frustration built in my chest.

"Force them back." If we couldn't take down the portal, maybe we could send them back through the bottleneck and hold them off that way.

Shadows crept to my feet and encircled my ankles. Celeste met my gaze and smirked as she blasted Shadows into the room. How was she this powerful? It must be the Heart of the Mountain. Our numbers were greater, and still, they held their own.

Cold bit into my skin with the Shadows. I jerked my foot away, and it wrapped around tighter, squeezing like a snake.

Enough.

I drew the dagger at my side and sent it end over hilt, ready to meet the dragon witch's heart. Faster than possible, even for a dragon, she wrapped her hand around the blade inches from her chest. Blood spilled down her forearm, and blue flames lit her eyes before they were replaced with Shadows.

The Shadows at my ankles pulled my legs out from beneath me and dragged me across the floor. My guards reached for me as I fell, but the Shadows ripped me from their grasp. I wrapped my hand around my second blade, ready to drive it through her heart.

The Shadows deposited me at Celeste's feet. She raised a brow. "Are you thirsty for my blood, High Queen?"

She lifted her hand and the Shadows wrapped their way around my torso, wispy but full of raw power. They pressed their way into my pores, looking for purchase in my soul. I knew the Shadows' ways and concentrated with everything in me not to feel the sting of ice or the pressure as they constricted.

Celeste leaned closer, her blood dripping on my legs. "I'm getting bored. Can you even rise?"

Sure and true, I stabbed toward her heart, ready to end this once and for all. A deep blue flame rose from my chest and burned my hand. The blade dropped. Flames exploded from my chest pushing Celeste away from me and I landed against the wall.

She crouched and whipped her honey-blond hair as she looked back at me. "How interesting." Her smile said it was anything but interesting. She knew something I had yet to piece together. What was it?

Shadows struck me, pinning me in place. I lifted my neck as they began to slither up to caress my throat. Fighting stopped around us—my clan was seeing my defeat.

Celeste rose upright in a slow stretch, her hand still controlling the Shadows around me.

"I'd say 'checkmate' since I have your queen, but that seems cheesy."

"When you kill me, there will still be those who oppose you," I began. "Killing me changes nothing. This clan belongs to the sea. She will choose a worthy dragon to raise up in my place."

"It won't matter if you are all under the rule of the Dragon King."

The portal flared to life behind her, and my lips twitched ever so slightly. "The Dragon King will not rule Sea clan. Neither will you."

Dark hair and eyes as blue as the sea, wild with fury, marched through the portal. Jenna sped to Celeste, grabbed her by her hair, and jerked her head back. Kipp moved through the portal, and the two locked white and red flames around Celeste.

I rose to my feet in time to see Samara pulling a body through the portal. The blond hair gave him away, and I rushed to help her. Tears poured down her face, her arms locked around the chest of her soulmate.

The Shadow dragons around us resumed their fighting, and with their queen free, the Sea dragons attacked with more fury.

I wanted to help, but Samara screamed anytime I tried to touch him. She pulled Simeon to the side of the room and let his body collapse on top of hers. Her hair cascaded over his face as she buried her head against his neck, her cries echoing out over the battle.

Jenna and Kipp forced Celeste back through the portal as she struggled against the flames of the rogue. Kipp ripped the seams out of the mirror as she disappeared into the dark of the portal.

My clan made quick work of the remaining Shadows, but all I could think was how were we going to survive the next time?

Chapter Twenty

Zale

"**B**uild up the magic around the walls."

"Go and attack the Dragon King now."

"Leave the humans to their fate."

I leaned forward on the throne, grasping the arms. A decision must be made, and the Mountain Queen was tending to her clan.

"I will take your words under advisement. For now, have our strongest dragons fortify the walls with their magic. Increase the patrols and call for all of Sea clan to gather at Firestorm."

"What of the Mountain clan?"

I stood and narrowed my eyes at the advisor. "I will discuss it with their queen."

"Their magic is weak. You cannot expect us to defend them."

"I do, and you will. I am still your High Queen."

I rose and left the room, eager to leave their prattle behind. Lance should return soon with Nyla, and then I could breathe easier. It was difficult to keep the cold, hard exterior I was used to without the power of my dragon flowing through me. I moved to my chambers, hoping Jenna was there with Jesse and Maddie. They were in the safest place in Firestorm, and I wouldn't have it any other way.

Jesse's face haunted my dreams even before I met Jenna. When I found him years ago, I thought he was Keani's child. It still concerned me that he continued to be in my visions. Sometimes he was thriving with his wife and daughter. Sometimes I saw his death. Humans would not survive the Dragon King, and I feared for his future.

Pushing open the door to my room, four sets of eyes turned to meet me.

"What happened, Jenna?"

"We were attacked. The Dragon King and his witch were waiting when we opened the portal."

My stomach clenched at how close Axel got to Firestorm. He was coming for me. It was only a matter of when.

"Casualties?"

Jenna's jaw clenched with her fists. "We lost a lot."

"I didn't see Travis and Ann..."

Jesse spoke up. "Our parents rejoined the Order. The need is greater than ever."

My eyes darted to how he stood in front of Maddie, half shielding her from my vision. "And you?"

"I continue to be a liaison between the Order and Mountain clan."

"I'll need you to be a liaison between Sea clan and the Order as well. We are all in this war together."

Jesse crossed his arms over his chest. "I'll speak with the general."

"See that you do it quickly. I'm expecting another attack."

Kipp spoke next. "How do you plan to hold them off?"

"It will only be a matter of time. I don't know how long we can hold them off. I plan to give them a fight when they do come. When he comes..." I turned to my cousin, knowing that she needed to be ready. "Jenna, when he does, you will have to lead."

"You can count on Mountain clan, Zale."

Sadness filled my chest. "That is not what I mean."

Jenna scrunched her face in confusion. She looked to Kipp and back to me. "Zale?"

"I...I was injured when the cord was cut. My dragon refuses to rise inside of me, choosing a cage of her own making in her grief."

"What of the Heart of the Sea?"

"The sea is fickle. She comes and goes as she pleases. I cannot rely on its magic."

Jenna stepped closer and placed her hand on my shoulder. "Zale, what are you trying to say?"

I scanned the faces of the ones I considered friends and family. "I am vulnerable. I have no access to magic. And...he is coming for me."

"We can protect you. There has to be a way, Zale."

I sighed. There was no way to explain my intuition to them. Axel would not rest until he had the Heart of the Sea, and so I knew he would come.

"Jenna. Promise me you will look after my clan."

"I'd rather promise to keep you safe. You protected me in the battle at Las Vegas. Let me return the favor."

Instead of answering, I opted for a different route. I looked to Jesse, hoping he could speak reason to his sister. "When you worked with Axel at the Order, did he give you any reason to believe he would not meet his goals? That he would fail?"

Jesse shifted his weight and crossed his arms. "No. Axel is singularly focused on his goals. He may hide his end game, but he always gets what he is after. Every single dragon we hunted, we found."

"Exactly. He is the same as he always has been. I would expect nothing less." I looked around the room and scanned for Simeon. "Where is Simeon? Samara? I thought they would be here."

"They're not here. Samara used her magic and took them away. And...Sim wouldn't wake."

I pulled my phone out and called his number. No answer.

I called Samara's phone. Again, no answer.

Chapter Twenty-One

Axel

The ache in my chest reminded me of who I was.

I was the Dragon King. I controlled magic in all its forms from the sea and the mountain. Somehow, that memory escaped me most days. The Shadows swarmed my mind, taunting me, forcing me to only see half the picture.

"We were so close to getting the stone, my love." Celeste snaked her arms around my shoulder from behind and pressed a delicate kiss against my neck. Her voice dripped like honey, and it took all of my self control not to tense when she touched me. There was a time when I welcomed her touch. That time was over. "Soon we will have it."

I put my hand on her arm and gave it a squeeze—the affectionate gesture was a common occurrence between us. For how long? I was not sure. I had to make sure she did not know. She couldn't know that I remembered who I was. She couldn't know that I was awake inside.

Shadows plucked at my memories, pulling the inconvenient ones and hiding the ones that set me free, but I held onto the ache. The one that woke me up.

Before, we believed that if the cord were severed, it would be easier to kill the High Queen. If she were dead, then we could take control of the Heart of the Sea, uniting magic. Celeste accused me of holding back when it came to my former soulmate.

She had no idea that severing the cord had stirred my memories. That the ache from where my soul was split in two made my mind sharp.

"And then?" I needed the reminder. The reminder of what she wanted from me.

"And then, you will be king." Her compliments evaded my question, frustrating me with every turn.

"I thought that I was already king?" I turned my head to meet her eyes, raising a brow.

She dragged her hand across my chest as she circled to the front of my desk. Pausing, she tilted her head and smiled. "You are, Axel. But once we have the Heart of the Sea, you will be king of *all* the dragons. No one can deny your power."

I studied her. How had she trapped me with the Shadows? It was so long ago, I could hardly remember. There was something...strange about this dragon. Perhaps it was the part of her that was a witch. Perhaps the two magics warred for control inside her. Perhaps they worked together. I wasn't quite sure. Either way, the magic was alluring to me. It captured my attention and drew me to her. Perhaps that was how she bound me in Shadows to begin with.

"Three times now, we have tried to claim the Heart of the Sea. It seems to be beyond our reach." I watched her face closely. She was lying to me, but about what? I chased down the thought, but it was fleeting and fell through my hand like water.

"I have a new plan, my love." Celeste settled her hips on my desk and slid closer as she twisted her body toward me. "We have been going about this all wrong. We have been trying to take the Heart of the Sea from the High Queen, but that seems to be the problem."

Her hair fell over her shoulder as she continued. "Who says we need to separate them? Why not bring the High Queen here? Away from her precious sea."

A grin tugged at my lips, and I allowed it. Celeste would think this was in agreement with her plan, but I had a plan of my own. If Zale were here, she would be an asset. I could use her to my own ends.

"Yes. I think that is an excellent idea. Make arrangements with our source. I want to be in Firestorm the day after next."

I stood and placed a brief kiss on her full lips. Not because I was compelled to, as I had been before, but because I needed her to believe me. To believe that she had blinded me to her plans. To believe that nothing had changed between us.

She stared back at me, her beauty failing to compare to my soulmate's. Was there anything that drew me to her? The Shadows twisted around my mind and brought back all the times I had her in my bed. I forced away the shudder that threatened to run through me.

As I walked away from my office and through Shadowkeep, I allowed the smile to pull at my face. The witch had no idea what cutting the cord did for me. She believed me to be as bound to her as ever before, through the Shadows. She would be furious when she realized that she had lost all that she worked so hard to gain. I tugged on the cuffs of my dress shirt, eager to be free of this charade.

It was true that the Shadows swarmed my mind still—that they manipulated and hid in the deepest recesses of my soul.

But now, the ache in my chest throbbed, outweighing the dark magic inside of me. It kept my mind sharp when the Shadows tried to sway it. Sadness rolled through me at the thought that I had lost my soulmate—the bond between us severed. I could not find it in myself to regret it though.

The ache is what reminded me of what I truly needed.

A savior.

Chapter Twenty-Two

Zale

When my phone rang, I expected it to be Simeon. Nyla spoke instead. "Zay, are you still at Firestorm?"

"Yes, I sent Lance for you days ago. Where are you?"

"I haven't seen him. I can come to you, though."

"Yes. Now."

"Zay...what's wrong?"

"I...need someone I trust."

Silence pulsed on the phone between us.

"I'll be there in an hour."

I clicked the phone off, my brow scrunched in confusion. Where was Lance? My eyes drifted closed, and I leaned back against the cushions of my bed. It would be so easy to let sleep take me.

The in-between gripped me, pulling me under—

I stood on the beach before Firestorm. The walls crumbled around me as the fortress blazed orange and red. A gust of wind hit my face, and I lifted my arm to shield my eyes. Hovering above my fortress was a black dragon with his chest scarred. With his wings outstretched, he narrowed his eye before roaring to the sky. The ground vibrated and trembled.

A voice whispered in my mind, "The end of the age of dragons."

Dragons with their scales torn and their bodies broken lay scattered at his talons. I lifted my arms and the sea raised her waves behind me, ready to wash him away. Then, I hesitated.

In the corner of the Dragon King's eye glistened a single tear.

I gasped as my mind jerked back to reality from the in-between. A prophecy. One that did not completely make sense, but the attack on my fortress was clear. I leaped to my feet and crossed the distance to my door.

"Kai, I need to assemble the advisors in the great hall. And call for the Mountain Queen." My guard dipped his head and headed off down the corridor.

I marched to my throne. How much time did we have? Best to assume we had none.

It haunted me that there was no connection to my dragon—that I couldn't defend my clan. As I sat on my throne, I wondered how it had come to the end—the end of the age of dragons.

"High Queen, what is the urgency?"

My advisors filtered into the room and I waited. Jenna needed to be part of this. If we were headed to the end, it would take every single one of us. Flashes of the black dragon hovering over the rubble of my sanctuary continued to speed in my mind. My chest ached, and I pressed my hand against the empty space where my cord once rested.

Did I mess this all up for everyone? Would every dragon be subjected to the Shadows because of my selfishness?

"Zale, what is it?"

Jenna's voice pulled me out of my thoughts, and I straightened in my throne.

"I have had a vision. The end of this war is near."

Kipp and Jenna shared a look. I scanned the room of advisors and warriors alike before I continued.

"I've seen the fall of Firestorm at the feet of the Dragon King. The end of the age of dragons."

"How do you know this?"

"How can you believe it is true?"

I held my hand up, and the room silenced. "I can not change the future, but I can prepare for it. I propose that we send our young ones out in groups with two warriors each. Scattering them across the earth will give them a chance to outlast the Shadows."

"You would have us hide?"

"No. I would have our most vulnerable hide. We will stand here." I gripped the arms of the throne. We didn't have time for more arguments.

Jenna stepped forward, her dark hair loose around her shoulders. "We will do as you have suggested. The rest of my warriors will stand with Sea clan."

"The Mountain warriors are weak. Their magic is lost to the Shadows. It would be better for them to run and hide as well."

I rose from my throne. "I will not have you dissenting my orders. The threat is obvious—The Dragon King and the Shadows. If you believe that dividing the clans will help, feel free to leave."

I let my words settle on them before I clasped my hands together, softening my posture. "Now, we can not hold off the Shadows without Mountain clan. We may not be able to do it even with their help. If the prophecy is correct, this is the final battle against the Dragon King. Let us make it one to remember."

Without allowing any other dragon to speak, I walked down the aisle of the great hall, motioning for Jenna to join me as I left. She fell into step beside me—two queens of a dying race.

"Zale," Jenna whispered.

"Not here."

We navigated the corridors of Firestorm in silence until we reached my rooms. I shut the door behind her.

"Zale, you should leave. If he is looking for you, perhaps that will draw his attention."

I shook my head. "He will come here regardless of if I'm here or not, Jenna. All that accomplishes is to extend his search. If we are to fall, I will do it here with my clan."

"Is that truly what your vision showed you? There has to be a way..."

I put my hand on her shoulders, an odd gesture for me to initiate, but Jenna's humanity was always more prevalent in her unwavering hope.

"There is not a way. He is coming. He will destroy Firestorm. Our clans will stand and...will likely fall."

A tear slipped down her cheek, and she quickly swiped it away. "This was not how I imagined my life."

I squeezed her shoulders. "No. I did not imagine a cousin on the throne of Mountain clan. Nor a friendship."

Jenna grinned and pulled me against her chest, squeezing tighter than necessary. When she finally released me, she went to the door. With her hand on the handle, she looked back.

"We will find a way to save our clans. A way to save *you*. I promise."

I held back the small sob until she closed the door behind herself.

There was no saving any of us.

Chapter Twenty-Three

Zale

T he door to my room burst open and Nyla rushed through it. "Zay. I'm here."

I sat up in the bed and swung my legs over the side. That's all I had time to do before she tackled me in a hug. I placed my hands delicately on her back.

"You're here."

Nyla released me and sat on the bed beside me. "What's going on, Zay? The whole fortress has a somber air about it."

"I...I had a vision. The Dragon King is coming."

Her eyes widened. "Then it's a good thing we are here. He can't possibly breach the walls with the amount of magic Sea clan has poured into it over the years."

I shook my head. "No. The vision was clear. He will succeed."

Nyla stood. "It's not possible." She began to pace in the room.

With a sigh, I rose and put myself in her path. "Nyla, have you heard from Lance? I called him twice and...I'm getting concerned."

She shook her head. "I called him too."

Where was he? He should be here. My mind raced at the possibilities.

The blaring alarms stopped my heart for a moment. We were under attack. I glanced at my friend. Her face dropped. "I thought we had more time?"

"What do you mean?"

Dark Shadows crept into my friend's eyes and rivers of ash crawled up her arms as the dark magic began to swirl around her.

"I'm so sorry, Zay. I...didn't have a choice."

My chest caved and I wasn't able to draw in a breath. My dearest friend...claimed by the Shadows.

"What did you do, Nyla?"

Tears fell on her cheeks and she shook her head. "I didn't want to. I couldn't stop it."

"What. Did. You. Do?"

"Please, forgive me."

The alarms blared louder as I backed away from my friend. Awareness dawned in my mind. "You brought them here?"

She nodded and choked out a sob. "He made me. I...When Lance found me..."

A tear slipped down my cheek and I stepped further away from her. A cold chill ran down my spine. "Lance? You..."

Nyla shook her head and the Shadows spiraled around her faster and faster until she was a blur in their center. "I...he saw...and I couldn't let you know I was coming..."

My hands came to my mouth and I shook my head, stepping closer to the door again. "Where is he, Nyla? Where is Lance?"

"D...dead."

My heart shattered into a million pieces. The world tilted on its axis again. This couldn't be happening. My best friend betrayed me and...murdered my Lance...

My hand landed on the door handle, and I flung it open. I had to get away. I yelped at Kai's broken body crumpled against the wall. Running with all the strength this human form held, I focused on the end of the hall. My arms pumped and my legs began to burn. Jesse walked into view in front of me. He lifted his hand, gun aimed behind me. Three shots echoed in the corridor. Jenna appeared at his side and let her white flames into the dragon behind me.

I stumbled as I reached them, refusing to look at my fallen friend, dead in the hall. Jesse pulled me behind him. "What is a Shadow dragon doing inside the fortress? How did she get here?"

"She...she was my...I trusted her." Tears slid down my face. Jenna took my arm and led me down the hall. I clung to her strength, my own failing me.

"Was she the only one?"

"No. We...need..."

Jenna put her fingers in her mouth and whistled. Two dark-haired Mountain warriors appeared. "We aren't dogs, Jenna. You can't just call us—"

"All warriors need to report to the great hall. Immediately."

"Kipp?"

"He is already aware. Jesse, you need to go."

Jesse put his hand on my shoulder before taking off down the hall. Jenna put her arm on my back and pulled me down the hall.

"Where is he going Jenna? He needs to be safe. And Maddie?" Fear climbed up my throat and threatened to choke me. I couldn't handle anyone else I loved being hurt.

"Samara is coming for them. She is going to protect them on Medney. We waited until the Shadows attacked so they would not be looking at the portals. Hopefully that will keep them secret. Safe."

"Simeon?"

Jenna glanced over at me before turning her eyes back on our destination. "He still will not wake."

I ran my hand over my hair. "And you? And Kipp? Where—"

"Don't do this, Zale. I am at your side to the end. If you say this is the end of dragons one more time, I swear I'll punch you. The Mountain Queen will be standing with you until the end."

I gripped her arm and slowed. "He only wants me. Take the dragons. Scatter. I'm the only one he wants."

"Not a chance. You asked me to lead and that's exactly what I will do."

"Please, cousin. I can't..."

Jenna put her hands on my shoulders and faced me again. "You can. You will. You are the High Queen. Keeper of the Heart of the Sea. You will not shrivel up and disappear. You will stand with your clan. We will stand together and face the end."

I bit my lip and nodded. Magic or not, friends or not, I was still the High Queen. I was still to lead. To sacrifice.

The ground beneath my feet vibrated and a thunderous roar filled the air.

I stared at Jenna's sea blue eyes.

"He's here."

Chapter Twenty-Four

Zale

We ran.

Down the corridor to the great hall, Jenna held herself back so I could keep pace. I steeled my heart against the grief and sadness I wanted to dwell in. I reached out to the sea as we ran, feeling her pulse around me—through me. My dragon continued to ignore my pleas to help, her heart too broken to care.

I scanned the great hall as we entered. There were too few of us. Even with the Mountain warriors, the Shadows would easily overwhelm us.

The walls of the fortress shook as another roar echoed in the air.

"Seal every entrance but this one. We will force them to attack here." I shouted my orders to the Sea guardsman.

I jogged up the steps to the throne and stood over my great hall, waiting, watching. I locked down my heart and mind. Nothing mattered but keeping them out of the great hall. Nothing mattered but keeping them from the Heart of the Sea. For as long as that was possible.

Kipp and Jenna stood on the steps before me—their joined flames spiraling and hovering, waiting to be used. My muscles twitched with anticipation. The silence before the battle was always the worst.

Cold crept up the back of my neck as the dark magic entered Firestorm. The Shadows were here.

My chest hummed with the Heart of the Sea. I begged the sea for her help to save my clan and the dragons.

The windows cracked and shattered as the wind stirred up the long curtains. The front of the great hall held my attention, and I ignored the chaos around me. A roar above the fortress sounded again as the ceiling trembled.

"Hold! Wait until you see them."

The wind grew chaotic and blew in several directions. Dragons with their flames at the ready waited for my orders.

The doors at the end of the great hall burst open, and Shadows and Shadow dragons poured inside.

"Attack!"

Dark magic spun around the room, and the battle began. In my heart and soul, I knew this was my last battle—the end of the age of dragons—and I wept. Tears streamed down my face, and I swiped them away.

Jenna and Kipp held back, shouting their orders and staying close to me. It was completely against my nature to let anyone protect me, yet I couldn't help but be thankful.

Celeste entered the great hall with her white dress whipping around her legs. Thigh-high cuts revealed her legs, and the Shadows slid around her limbs—climbing and dancing with her as she moved. Her eyes met mine, and she grinned.

I pulled on the magic that rested in my chest. The Heart of the Sea refused my call. I begged and begged for it to help us. To destroy her and the Shadows. Why did the sea reject me now when I needed it the most?

Debris fell from the ceiling. The Dragon King's black talons extended the hole he ripped in my fortress. I moved from the podium, shielding my head as I moved. Jenna grabbed my arm and pulled me to the back wall.

She put herself between me and the Shadows, sending her white and red flames into each one that approached. They moved with one motive—to get to me, making their intentions clear.

Celeste continued to stare at me like a trophy. If my dragon would respond, I would wipe that smile clean off her face.

The Dragon King pushed his head through the hole in the ceiling and roared.

I covered my ears, and Jenna mouthed the one word I wanted to refuse. "Run!"

With grace, my cousin shifted as easily as if she were always a dragon and hadn't spent her entire childhood among humans. Her scales glittered against the flames of the room. She positioned her body between me and the Dragon King, spreading her wings and knocking over several columns in the room. Her giant tail lashed at the back wall, creating an opening for me.

Tears flowed freely now, and I covered my head as I sprinted through the rubble to the ocean, praying she would save me. And if she wouldn't, maybe she would take back her heart.

The shifting of many dragons echoed behind me. I turned on the beach and stared at Firestorm.

Flames of every color lit up my fortress. The bodies of my dragons fell from the sky as Shadows consumed them. Shadow dragons moved to my dragons one by one and destroyed them.

I scanned the area for Jenna. She needed to retreat—to escape.

I couldn't lose anyone else.

A scarred red dragon appeared on the beach in front of me. His white and red flames gave away his identity. Kipp stood between me and the Dragon King. I backed step by step down the beach until I stood in the waves, the surf licking around my thighs and yet continuing to ignore my request for help.

The Dragon King landed before Kipp and snapped at his neck, testing his defenses. Kipp evaded with ease. He whipped his tail at Axel's legs. Axel lifted up on his back legs and let out a flame so intense I shielded my face from yards away.

Kipp roared and released flames of his own in an arc across the sky. Axel launched at Kipp with grace and speed, clamping down on his wing.

Kipp's howls echoed off my fallen fortress, and I covered my mouth.

Jenna dove out of the air and knocked the Dragon King off her soulmate. Axel swiped his talons through her exposed underbelly. He kicked her away, and her body tumbled down the beach against the surf-slapped rocks.

I screamed her name, begging her to get up. Her body remained still on the sand.

Kipp stumbled and shifted. He turned, and his eyes met mine the moment before they rolled back in his head and he fell to the ground.

No.

No.

"No!"

Anger and fury flowed easily through me. The water vibrated in response to my emotions. I wanted to drown the entire fortress, but the sea wouldn't listen. I wanted to drown the Dragon King, and the sea abandoned me.

Everyone I loved.

Everyone I cared about was gone.

And there was nothing I could do to fix it.

Axel shifted and tugged on his cuffs as he approached me in the water. I met his eyes and saw a single tear glistening in the corner of his eye. Shadows swarmed around him, and he put his arms around me.

"I've got you now."

His tone didn't match the menace those words should carry. He said them low like a lover in my ear.

The Shadows swirled around us, and darkness took hold.

The end of the age of dragons, indeed.

Chapter Twenty-Five

Zale

When my eyes opened, it was as dark as if I had never opened them. I blinked and reached for my head. It ached and pulsed.

I touched the back of my head. No injuries.

Why did my head hurt so much?

I reached out to my dragon, and she remained curled in a cage of her own grief.

I listened around me in the pitch black of night. Nothing stirred. Nothing but my own movements and breathing echoed around me. My fingers ran along the edges of the surface I laid on. Stone covered by a thin mattress.

Slowly the darkness began to vary, and I could make out the bars a few feet away. I ran my tongue over my cracked lips. How long had I been here?

I swung my legs over the side of the cot, and metal clanked. Heavy metal pressed against my ankle, scraping the skin. I followed the metal links with my fingers to the stone wall. Another cage. Another chain. I pulled on it, but it remained firmly in place.

My stomach rumbled, and I wrapped my arms around my waist, pressing firmly to offset the pain from the hunger and thirst. If I could only have some water, I would be able to think more clearly.

Memories of the battle of Firestorm played over and over in my head. How the sky darkened with the Shadows and how my clan fell to the dark magic.

Jenna's broken dragon haunted my mind. If the Mountain Queen were really dead, there would be no one to lead, and dragons were not easy to tame. There would be no one to bring them together and fight back against the Shadows.

I rolled my neck and pressed my fingers against the tight muscles. Why was I lying to myself? She could not have survived. And her joined soulmate fell. Their magic would have made one's fate the other's as well. There was no more Mountain Queen. No more...Jenna.

I swiped the tears away from my cheeks, sucking in a shaky breath.

Simeon was still lying unconscious on his island, his soulmate desperate to protect him and Maddie. They were sitting ducks. At least he had stored many magics and laid many traps over the last few years. How long until the Shadows sought them out and destroyed them, too?

Nyla's betrayal burned hotter in my chest. It was almost enough to stir up my dragon. Almost. She was my confidant. She brought the dragons to me. How had the Shadows turned her? She was supposed to be bound to me. Somehow, they still reached her.

Lance...my friend. My—he was gone. There would be no goodbye. No conclusion to our story and that part burned the hottest. He loved me and we never even had a chance.

And my clan? Lost and scattered. At least they would be, if they weren't already dead. I failed them. I...lost.

I dropped my face in my hands and wept. How had we gotten to this point?

How had I gotten here?

This wasn't what was supposed to happen.

We were supposed to win—to destroy the Dragon King. To free dragons. That's what the visions showed once before.

I let the waves of emotions wash over me.

It wasn't worth all my pain and suffering. It wasn't worth the years I stayed silent and endured the abuse. It wasn't worth the years I denied anything for myself.

How was I supposed to know that putting on the show for everyone to keep the Heart of the Sea safe wouldn't be worth it?

It wasn't worth the not living.

If we had won against the darkness, then maybe it would have been.

I wrapped my hands around my waist and wailed, tears falling harder. My heart fractured into too many pieces to count. My soul shredded and fell away from my body. My dragon retreated from me, hiding in her grief.

For too long, I kept secrets.

For too long, I held inside what should have been said.

Did Jenna know that I loved her?

Did Simeon?

I missed out on years of loving Lance out of fear that he would be harmed, only to lose him anyway.

I lost my dragon.

I lost my clan.

I lost my crown.

I lost my soulmate.

My voice lifted, and I called for the ocean to come to me. Maybe she could wash away the tears of a dragon. Maybe she could take these fractured, shattered pieces of my heart and make them whole. Maybe she could make this...better.

She did not answer my call.

She did not hear it.

Wherever I was, I was locked deep and far away from any water.

Inside my chest, I held the Heart of the Sea, and yet I was so far from her she couldn't hear me.

My wails settled into soft sobs. The numbness settled around my heart, attempting and failing to make this easier. No one was coming for me. No one could help me. I was well and truly alone now.

Or so I thought.

The clang of metal echoed around the stone and I lifted my head.

I wasn't alone.

Chapter Twenty-Six

Zale

"H...hello?"

A groan emitted from the darkness.

I rose and walked as close to the bars as my chain would allow. "Hello? Do you need help?"

A wry chuckle rose in my throat. I couldn't help myself, much less someone else.

Another groan sounded against the stone walls. "Are you injured?"

The clinking of metal was the only reply. I waited and waited, but still nothing but the sound of the metal echo on the walls. After what seemed like an eternity, a voice, low and raspy, called out. "I didn't know anyone else was alive down here."

"Where exactly are we?" I leaned against the cell bars to see if I could make out the form of the person speaking.

"I'm not sure. Time seems to move at a different pace these days."

"What do you mean?"

"Are you not also fighting the Shadows?"

"I'm not fighting the Shadows because I've already lost to them."

"You say you have lost, but you do not sound like they are consuming you." The prisoner groaned again.

"I do not suffer from the dark magic. I have only lost against it."

Metal rattled again, and I began to see a form sitting on the floor across the narrow hallway.

"What have you lost?"

I pondered what I could tell him. I could tell him that I had lost my crown, my clan, my friends, my family, but the words failed me.

"Everything," I whispered.

The stranger chuckled. "You still have your freedom." His words sounded more like an accusation than a comment.

"Freedom? We are in a prison."

"Freedom from the Shadows. You have your mind. You have your heart and your soul. You do not have to worry about those things."

Silence filled the space. There was no way to answer him. I had my mind, my fractured heart, and my battered soul. He was right.

"What is your name? Why are you here?"

Another grown came from across the hall, and I saw the figure lean against the iron bars. "I was once called Marcos."

"Are you human?"

"No, the humans cannot be controlled by the Shadows. Only dragons."

"If you are a dragon, what clan do you come from?"

"Mmmm...Mountain clan, but it seems so long ago."

The dragon coughed and hacked, his chains rattling as he did. When he finally regained his composure, he began to ask the questions.

"You are not from Mountain clan, and you do not have the Shadows. Are you human?"

"No." It would've been simpler if I were human, not the dethroned royal I was.

"Then you are from the mighty Sea clan. Tell me, have the Shadows infiltrated their ranks yet?"

"How long have you been here? Yes. Many Shadow dragons are from Sea clan."

He cleared his throat. "I heard a rumor about a Sea dragon once. They called her Tiamat. They called her a savior."

I remain silent for a time before answering him.

"Tiamat grieves. She has locked herself away in a cage of her own making."

"Then, I am truly sorry. I had hoped that there would be some saving for us."

I moved back to my cot and held my head in my hands. How has my name reached so far into the Shadows' depths that even this prisoner knew who I was? It didn't change anything. I wasn't who he thought I was. Not anymore.

A light bounced off the walls of the corner, and I heard footsteps. I raised my head and watched and waited until Celeste stepped in front of the bars.

"Good evening, High Queen. I was wondering if we could have a chat?"

"I have nothing to say to you."

"Oh, I think you will." Celeste waved her arm, and the iron doors swung in. She placed her hand delicately on her hip, watching me. Shadows danced around her arms, sneaking their way up around her shoulders.

"I hope you don't mind, Marcos, but I have to chat with the queen. It won't bother you if she screams, will it?"

I narrowed my eyes at the dragon witch. "I have never screamed under torture before, and I don't intend to now."

Light illuminated my cell from every angle. I raised my arm to shield my eyes and stepped back toward the wall.

"Now, is that any way to treat our guest Celeste?"

Axle's broad frame stepped into my cell behind Celeste. His steel gray eyes scoured my face, and I wanted to look away, but I lifted my chin instead. I may be a prisoner, but I was still...me.

"I'm hardly a guest with chains around my ankles."

"I could call you a trophy, but I was trying to be polite."

"What you call me makes no difference to me."

Celeste reached out her hand palm up between us. "Give me the stone, and I'll be gone."

"No." It was the easiest thing I had said all night.

Celeste looked over at Axel and grinned. "Oh, good. She wants to do this the hard way."

With the slow grace of a seductress, she turned her gaze back to me. Her outstretched hand twisted, and she released vivid blue flames directly at my chest.

My back slammed into the stone wall, and my head cracked against it. She continued to hold the blue flames to my chest—their heat calling to the Heart of the Sea. They could only do that if...

"How? How are you, one of us? I know all of Sea clan."

"I'm afraid you do not, High Queen. In fact, you and I are related."

I groaned under the flames as they licked the skin away from my chest. "It's not possible. I know all of the royal line. You're not in it."

Celeste's smile widened. "How do you suppose one becomes a dragon witch?"

"Is that a trick question, Celeste? Get on with it." Axel jerked his chin in my direction.

Celeste chuckled, and she increased the intensity of her flames into my chest. "Well, I will give you a hint. My mother was a witch, so who do you suppose my father was?"

I ground my teeth together, focusing all of my energy on ignoring her flames.

"My father was Julian Silva, High King of Sea clan."

My stomach dropped at my grandfather's name, and I realized that she must be telling the truth. Her blue flames marked her as my clan. And the Heart of the Sea was pushing out of me...to her. It must be why the stone would not help me to destroy her. She was part of the sea.

"You cannot have it. The sea gave it to me."

Celeste struggled to bring the stone out of my chest, and I fought with everything in me to keep it inside. When the stone didn't go to her, Celeste pulled a knife from her waist and approached me. Her Shadows restrained me to the wall, and she brought the knife down to where the stone rested.

"If you do not give it to me, I will have to take it."

Deep blue flames flashed out of me as the tip of her knife rested against my skin and knocked her away.

Sweat dripped off my brow, and I pulled air into my lungs, exhausted from the effort to resist. My chest ached and stung where new skin knit itself back together.

Axel offered his hand to Celeste, and she gracefully allowed him to help her to her feet.

"There is no rush, Celeste. The High Queen is not going anywhere. You'll find a way," Axel placed his hand on her back and guided her out of the cell.

She glared as she and Axel exited down the corridor, taking the light with them.

"Yes. I will."

Chapter Twenty-Seven

Zale

I needed a way out. The darkness pressed in around me, and I paced back and forth along the edge of the cell.

I had to get out. A cell so deep I couldn't even *feel* water was unbearable. There should have been moisture somewhere in these depths, but if there was, it wasn't responding to me.

"You're pacing again," Marcos called out from his cell.

"I have nothing else to do."

"Are you sure? You could give me your name?"

"No, that is not going to help. I need to find a way out."

"I already told you, High Queen, there is no way out."

"Maybe not for you, but I won't stay in a prison. I lived in one for too long already."

"A queen in a prison? Now that sounds like a story."

I crossed my arms over my chest and let out a breath. "It's not a happy story."

"Well, we're not exactly going anywhere now, are we?"

The metal links clicked together as I went to sit on my stone cot. We weren't going anywhere. What was the harm in sharing information in the depths of a prison?

"My...my father was not kind. Nor was my grandfather. They did not know what to do with me."

"I don't understand. Wouldn't they want to teach you how to be a queen?"

"No. They were more concerned with ensuring I didn't follow in my aunt's footsteps. She was more wild than the rest of us. Keani came and went as she pleased. My grandfather and my father believed it was what got her killed."

"And you act like your aunt?"

"In many ways, yes."

"You don't have to be secretive with me. I'm not going to tell anyone."

"I guess you already know about the Heart of the Sea." I weighed the choices in my mind and decided to tell Marcos my story. "My aunt passed it to me right before she died. She said I was the only one left with the deep magic—magic that is sacred to the sea. The Heart of the Sea stays inside me, but I do not control it. I only protect it.

"I'm not sure if it is the stone or part of my own magic, but I hear a voice in my mind. It begs me to wander. To keep moving. To go north."

"And your grandfather and father did not like this?"

"They did not. Partly because they did not know where I was, but mostly because they could not control me."

"So they locked you up?"

"They put me in prison. And when that didn't work, they tortured me. They would beat and whip me while I rested in golden chains. They believed that I was unable to defend myself, and I let them...all to keep the Heart of the Sea a secret."

"And you still ended up here."

"And I still ended up here. That's why I have to escape. I need to find my clan. I need to wander."

I grabbed hold of the metal links and yanked against them again, but without my dragon, it was pointless. I screamed at the ceiling in frustration. There was a point in my life where I chose to stay in chains that I could remove. It was infuriating to be forced to stay in chains I could not.

"What about you, Marcos? What story do you remember about yourself?"

"I believe I was a warrior...a Mountain warrior."

"Do you have any stories about your battles?"

"No, I hardly remember my time at Desmond's side. I was... His guard? I think?"

"The Mountain King? You were his guard?"

"I...I think so. It all seems so far away."

"Do you remember a guard named Kipp? He, too, served with Desmond."

"No...perhaps if I saw his face..."

"You know...Desmond and my aunt had an affair."

"No. It doesn't sound like Desmond. He was proud and fierce. He loved our clan. At least that's how I remember him."

A smile formed on my face. They should be commended for their secrecy. No one would have believed it without Jenna. "There's living proof...Well, there was. They had a daughter."

I sucked in a breath and held back the tears. They didn't do me any good here. I pushed down all the memories of Jenna and the joy she brought to my soul. I shoved away the grief that threatened to paralyze me. Remembering Jenna would have to wait.

"What...what else do you remember, Marcos?"

"The Festival of Dreams." I heard the smile in his voice.

"Tell me about it. I've never been."

"You wouldn't have been, High Queen. Dreaming belongs to the mountains."

I laughed loudly at his statement. "That's hardly true. The sea brings me many dreams."

He paused, and after a few moments, he began again. "Are you...are you Tiamat, High Queen? The rumors say Tiamat sees prophecies in her dreams and that she saves dragons from the Shadows."

There wasn't any point in hiding it any longer. "I was, Marcos. But I made a mistake, and now my dragon refuses to acknowledge me."

"What mistake did you make, Tiamat?"

My mind revisited the night I stood before Axel in the cemetery and all the reasons I chose to cut our cord. At the time, it seemed like the only choice. Now? Would I go back and change that? I wasn't sure.

"I traded an evil soulmate for the possibility of a future. And I lost."

Chapter Twenty-Eight

Zale

Days passed, and we saw no one. At least, it appeared to be days. My stomach had long ceased rumbling and moved on to painful cramping.

I touched the stone of my cell, trying and failing to find any water to call to my aid. Or for Marcos. His breathing often stilled for so many moments I believed him gone, only to have him gasp and breathe again. How much time did he have left?

Our conversations were few and far between. When he did speak, nightmares appeared to be what he was seeing. My heart ached to help him, to set him free, but I couldn't do that without water. And my dragon. She lifted her head a few times at my begging but returned to ignoring me.

I dreamed as I drifted asleep. The in-between seemed different—darker somehow. Keani did not meet me. The ancestors drifted closer at times than they ever had before. The waves came onto the beach, but I could never touch them. I cried trying to reach the water, but my feet remained firmly in place. Visions of destruction and the world burning flashed around me, making it impossible to rest.

Something nudged my leg and my eyes shot open.

"Stand up." Axel stepped back and crossed his arms over his chest.

"I don't take orders from you."

"I am your king."

"Not mine. I don't enslave those I lead. Nor do I bow to those who do."

Axel reached down and grabbed my arm, pulling me to my feet. He sent white flames into the chains that connected me to the wall, shattering them, and dragged me into the hall.

"Let me go." My voice was painfully weak, even in my own ears.

He raised a brow. "No."

His grip loosened slightly, but he continued to pull me down the corridor. "Where are you taking me?"

"I'm allowed to see my trophies whenever I want, and I want to now."

I jerked my arm, attempting to break his hold and failing. "I am no one's trophy."

"I would beg to differ, princess, but a king begs no one."

My chains rattled, and I struggled to keep pace with him, but I was grateful for my body's endurance. Shadow dragons lined the halls at each corner we turned, and my soul wept at all those enslaved to the dark magic. Anger burned hot in my belly at the dragon who dared to treat his species like this.

We entered a room with a long table with place settings at two seats. Axel deposited me in a seat where there was no plate. He sat at the head of the table and pulled on the cuffs of his shirt.

I glared as my stomach awoke and began to rumble. The table held foods of all kinds, but I smelled the water. My dragon lifted her head, and my gold tattoos flashed across my skin. I pulled my hands under the table, hoping to keep them out of sight.

Axel glanced over, but if he saw them, he said nothing.

Why had he brought me here?

He wanted the Heart of the Sea, but why bring me *here*?

The doors at the other end of the room burst open, and Celeste marched in. Her red dress flowed behind her as she moved. "I didn't know you were bringing a guest, my love."

"I didn't know I needed your permission." Axel cut into his food, failing to look up.

Celeste turned her gaze from him to me. With a delicate grace, she slipped into the seat at Axel's side. "Is there something the High Queen needs to say? Does she want to negotiate?"

"No. I do not."

Axel looked up at me as he grinned. "I wanted to see my trophy. Isn't that enough of a reason?"

Celeste placed her fingers on his arm and leaned closer to him. "I see no reason she needs to be brought here. She's filthy. She's our prisoner."

Axel put down his silverware and patted Celeste's hand. "She is *my* prisoner. I will do with her as I please."

"Of course, my love." I watched as she pulled her hand back to her lap, waiting to see how she would respond. It seemed to be a battle of their wills, and I could not quite understand the hidden meaning behind their words.

Axel pushed a crystal glass filled with water in front of me. "Drink."

My eyes darted to him, but he continued on with his meal. Celeste watched him intently as he ate. Was this a trap? Some poison to force me to release the stone?

In the end, it was my dragon who lifted her head and convinced me to drink.

My fingers gripped the glass, and I tilted the rim against my lips. Precious water flowed into my mouth, and I swallowed with greed.

When the glass was empty, I set it on the table and Axel filled it from a pitcher again.

He slid the glass in front of me, and as I reached for it, our fingers brushed. I pulled back my hand and watched him. His eyes never met mine. He released the glass and continued his meal.

"This is not what we talked about, my love."

Axel slammed his fist onto the table. "Last time I checked, I was the Dragon King. Not you."

Celeste stood, an air of purpose circling around her. "You are king. I have things to attend to."

Her dress flowed like fire as she left the room.

The entire conversation remained a mystery to me. I glanced around again for more clues as to what I was missing, but the truth evaded me.

I lifted my glass again to my lips, and as the water hit my tongue, my dragon lifted her magic and filled me once more. It took all of my restraint to keep from coughing or reacting at all. She hovered below my skin, seeping her purpose into my mind and soul with deep intention.

Free them.

Free them all.

I set the glass down on the table, and for the briefest of moments, it appeared that Axel was smiling. When he finally lifted his face to me, his features had hardened again.

"Maybe if you ask nicely, princess, I'll let you have something to eat."

"That's not necessary."

"Surely you are hungry."

I remained silent, afraid my dragon would respond and give me away.

Stay hidden. Let us choose the moment we reveal ourselves.

Axel rose from his seat. "Well, if you are not hungry, then perhaps you should return to your accommodations."

He turned his back and strolled out of the room, two Shadow dragons entering in his place. They took my arms and guided me back to my cell.

I waited right until they began to open my cell door.

And then I placed my hands on their chests and searched out the Shadows. My dragon sprung to life inside me. The deep magic hummed and hissed as the water left my body to purge theirs. I pulled Shadows out of their eyes and mouths. I pulled them out of their minds and hearts. And when those parts were clean, I reached down into their souls and pulled all the Shadow away.

It took every drop of water inside me that I had to spare. My lips bled. My skin grew taut. My eyes became uncomfortable.

Chains rattled in the cell across the hall.

"Tiamat..."

When I was finished, both dragons stared at me, confusion written on their faces.

"What...? How...?"

My lips curved up for the first time in what felt like a lifetime. "Hello. My name is Tiamat."

Chapter Twenty-Nine

Zale

The two dragons stared at me with wide eyes.

"Go," I told them. "Continue with what you're doing."

"But the Shadows... How did you—"

"It does not matter now." I pulled my own cell door shut, pushing them out into the hallway. "Go."

"What do you need? How can we help?"

"The best thing you can do is to continue your duties and remember what happened. I will need allies ahead."

The two began to leave but paused when I spoke again. "And water. If you can bring me water, I can recover."

"Recover?"

"Taking Shadows from a dragon is not easy."

Marcos groaned again, and the chains rattled.

"Go," I told them.

The two dragons scurried down the corridor. The wooden door echoed loudly as it closed.

"Tiamat...I thought you didn't have access to your dragon."

"She changed her mind."

I took a deep breath and sat on the stone cot, wondering what I should do next. The entire fortress was covered in Shadows, and I was weak.

I lifted my arms and let the blue flames spiral around them—my tattoos hovering just above my skin. The warmth of the flames invigorated my soul.

I wanted to shift and feel the air move over my wings, to feel my scales in the ocean again.

It would have to wait. There were dragons that needed saving, and I needed a plan.

"Why do you think she came back?" The raspy voice broke my train of thought

"I...I don't know. Maybe it was seeing all of the enslaved dragons. Maybe it was because she realized I was truly alone. Either way, I'm grateful."

The creak of the wooden door at the end of the hall sounded again. I rose to my feet, expecting the two dragons I had healed. Honey-blond hair and a red flowing dress met me instead.

"I have an idea, and I'll need you to come with me." Celeste waved her hand, and the cell door swung open. "If you try to resist me, I'll kill him." Celeste gestured to Marcos behind her. Could she hear our conversations? Did she know or was she playing on my need to help others? I nodded and stepped out of the cell. She gripped my arm and pulled me down the corridor.

"I'm thinking that the reason the stone won't leave you is because you don't have any water. Our king gave me an idea when he was allowing you to drink. Perhaps if you have water, then you can release the stone."

"The stone chose me. I did not choose this."

"Then you can release it."

"If I could release it on my own, I would've done so a long time ago, but the Heart of the Sea chose me. And now, there is no way I will give it to you."

"We'll see about that."

Celeste brought me to a courtyard filled with stone statues. Snow fell from a gray sky, and I shivered as the cold wind hit my face. How far away from the sea were we?

"These are hot springs. It's not the sea, but it'll have to do."

The witch dragged me into the heated waters and plunged my head below the surface. My dragon roared inside me, but I warned her to stay silent. We needed our secret.

I gasped for air when Celeste finally pulled me out from under the water. She pressed her hand to my chest and whispered words from the old script. Her Shadows pinned my arms to my sides.

The Heart of the Sea began to glow under my skin, and it warmed under her touch. I held myself in check, restraining my newly recovered magic.

"It belongs to me. It is my birthright. Not yours."

A grin slipped on my face. "If it were yours, it wouldn't be living inside my chest."

Her face soured in concentration, and she scratched at the skin on my chest, trying to get to the stone. I pushed against the Shadows until I could escape and staggered back from her.

"You can't take it from me, and you can't kill me. The Heart of the Sea is the reason I can't kill you. It won't let us destroy each other because you are my blood—my clan. You will have to accept this."

"I don't accept it! I will find a way to get the stone." Her eyes became wild as she spoke.

"It's not yours to take." I pushed my way through the waters toward the snowy bank.

Celeste sent Shadows around my waist and throat, pulling me back to her. I clutched and pushed at the dark magic but failed to escape it. She leaned closer, and her lips brushed my ear as she spoke.

"My dragon's fire may not be able to take the stone, but the Shadows are different. They do not care about their host."

The Shadows tightened around my throat and seeped into my skin. The dark magic suffocated me, trying to find a way into my soul. I looked up at the sky, wondering how long until I released my dragon to do her work. While I stared above me, I spied two black jets crossing the sky seconds before the explosions began, and Celeste dropped me back into the water.

Chapter Thirty

Zale

The explosion shattered stone everywhere. Bits of debris cut through the water, and sliced through my skin. My blue flames spiraled around my body and healed each cut as they came.

I lifted my head out of the water to a completely different scene than the one I saw before I submerged. The sky filled with smoke and ash. Many Shadow dragons had shifted, while others remained in human forms on the ground. The beasts flew over the fortress in every direction, their ashy wings spread as they roared and snapped at the helicopters.

Dozens of humans parachuted out of planes and landed in the courtyard and outside of the fortress, each one heavily armed. I could barely make out the red armbands as they drifted to the ground.

Knights.

"Come on, princess. Can't have you running off in the scuffle."

Behind me, Axel held out his hand on the bank. Ignoring his outstretched hand, I climbed out of the water on my own. My skin soaked in the water and my dragon breathed a sigh of relief.

"Afraid your trophy is going to disappear?"

He stood and grinned. "No, but I'll keep you close all the same."

Axel put his hand on my lower back and guided me into Shadowkeep while dragons fought against the humans. He moved with purpose but did not hurry, completely unbothered that his home was under attack.

"Where is your witch?"

"She is dealing with the nuisance on the front lawn."

"I'd hardly call humans a nuisance. You should be careful, Your Majesty. I've heard they've killed dragons."

He glanced at me before returning his gaze to our destination. "This will all be over in a moment."

"How wonderful." I straightened my back and quickened my steps so his hand no longer needed to rest against me.

He caught up to me in the hall. "Ready to be rid of me so soon?"

"I have no reason to speak with you. No reason to need your presence."

"Oh, no? I am your king."

I spun and faced him. "I've told you before, you are not my king. I am a prisoner here. I do not owe you my loyalty. I do not owe you my life. I do not owe you anything."

"What about answers? Do you owe me those?"

"No. I do not."

I turned to continue walking down the hall, when he caught my elbow. "What about the cord?"

I lifted my brow. "What about it? It's cut. Severed. There's nothing else to say."

"Why did you do it?"

I scanned his face. What was he doing? Why was he asking?

First the water. Now this.

Pulling my arm away from his grasp, I stepped away from him. "I did it for a chance at a future. I did it for my clan."

"And what of me, princess? What do you think of me now?"

"What does it matter, Axel? I'm a prisoner. We will not agree. And to be frank, you're a little busy right now. If you didn't notice, your home is being invaded."

Echoes of gunshots and yells from both dragons and humans bounced around the hall, but he ignored them. "Do you regret it? Cutting our cord?"

I lifted my eyes to his silver ones, trying to understand his game. It unsettled me to not know what his intentions were. "No. I don't regret it."

The corners of his lips lifted into a smile. "Neither do I."

He put his hand on my lower back again and guided me down the hall. "Now, I have something that I need to take care of before I return you to your accommodations."

"You could let me find my own way back. I'm sure I won't get lost."

Axel turned his head to glance at my face before looking forward again. "I'm sure. I'd rather escort you given our intruders."

I took a deep breath to settle my emotions as we walked. He wasn't my soulmate any longer. He shouldn't have this effect on me. The spot where his hand touched my back burned hot and I was overly sensitive to his scent surrounding us in the hall. My eyes wanted to sneak glances at his face, but I held them steady in front of us.

It was easy to speak with him. And it was rare for me to not fully understand another dragon. Discernment was part of the deep magic.

So why was he so difficult to read?

He opened the door and led me inside, where Shadow dragons surrounded a group of humans. Each of them was stripped of their weapons and held their hands to the back of their heads. Their eyes jumped to us when we entered the room.

"We gathered as many as we could, Your Majesty."

"Good. Thank you." Axel dropped his hand from my back and straightened his sleeves. "What to do with them though..."

I turned to see him, and he seemed to be waiting on me to speak.

"If you are asking me, I would release them. They are not a threat without their weapons."

It was foolish to think he would actually let them free, but I wasn't going to waste a chance to help the humans.

Axel waved his hand in the air. "You heard her. Release them. Show them out the back though so the witch doesn't notice, hmm?"

"Your Majesty?" The Shadow dragons looked at each other in confusion.

"You heard me."

He put his hand on my back and turned me again, leading us back into the hall.

"What was that? Are they going to be all right?"

"Hmm?"

"You...just let them go."

Without looking at me once, he responded. "I did."

"Why?"

Only the sound of our footsteps echoed in the hall. His hand pressed more firmly against my back, and he leaned closer, whispering low so no one would hear.

"Because you asked it."

Chapter Thirty-One

Zale

"Here, I bought you more water." She shoved the pitcher through the cell bars.

"Thank you, Julie. I appreciate this, but you don't have to keep sneaking it here. I don't want you to be at risk."

"You need more. I'll be bringing more Shadow dragons later."

I passed the pitcher back to her. "Give some to Marcos please."

"I don't need it, Tiamat." His voice sounded worse than normal.

"You do." It broke my heart that I couldn't get to him. Celeste and Axel seemed to be the only ones with access to unlock my cell or his. I couldn't reach him to heal him. "I need you strong for when I pull the Shadows from you."

Julie crossed to the opposite cell and handed the worn dragon water. He struggled to hold the pitcher and Julie helped him the best she could. He dragged his feet a little bit closer, and the chains rattled louder. My heart broke a little more with each sound.

"What is happening in Shadowkeep, Julie?"

She glanced at me over her shoulder. "The king has ordered a search for all dragons. He wants every dragon to be found and brought here. He wants them bound to the Shadows."

"Do they know where the dragons are?"

She shook her head. "They seem to be scattered. There are rumors of dragons in the Himalayan Mountains, but no confirmed reports yet."

Marcos coughed and Julie returned her attention to helping him. In the darkness, his eyes met mine. He knew something, but chose not to say it aloud.

"Do you know what he wants with the dragons?"

"The witch said they plan to give them the Shadows. Beyond that, I do not know."

I nodded. This was the plan all along for them. Unite dragons under the dark magic. If only we could have united ourselves sooner, maybe we would have had a chance against the Shadows. It was just another way I had failed my clan.

"And does anyone suspect you? I can't have you compromised either."

"No, Tiamat. No one suspects me."

"Please stay discreet. Once I am discovered, it will be impossible for me to help anyone else."

"You have my word."

Julie gathered the pitcher and the glass and disappeared into the darkness. When the door closed behind her, I moved to the bars of my cell. The shackles scraped against my ankles and chaffed as I moved.

"Marcos, what do you know?"

He moaned and the chains rattled again. "There is a secret stronghold for Mountain clan in the Himalayas. It can only be accessed by portal and Mountain magic. It's possible that they would use it now. Although it would still be risky since the witch has the Heart of the Mountain."

My heart skipped and I wondered if it were possible that dragons were able to gather together. *What if Jenna—*

I cut the thought off before I could let it take root. This was not a time to hope. It was only information. Information that wouldn't help me unless I could escape.

My mind and heart battled about whether I would be more helpful to my clan here or out in the world searching. Here I could save those already enslaved. Out there, I would have to find them first. And while I might know where to find the Mountain dragons, where would my clan hide with our Firestorm destroyed?

I pondered for many hours on where they would be, and what my best options were before the door creaked open again. White fire gave away the king as he stormed down the hall. He wasn't exactly being discreet, though.

"Hello, princess. I've decided to give your rooms an upgrade." He swung the door to the cell open.

"What do you mean?"

"I don't think it's fitting that a queen rots in my prison." He knelt before me and sent fire into the shackles that held me. "I have no reason to fear you, so I should be more accommodating."

"I don't mind the prison." My heart raced at the thought of leaving Marcos down here without having freed him.

"Don't be silly." He grabbed my arm and pulled me out into the hall. He jerked me closer and lowered his voice. "If you're going to be reckless, I want you doing it close to me."

I steeled my face and told my heart to keep beating. What did he know? "Reckless?"

Axel scoffed and began to guide me down the hall. "And you think I'm the one playing games."

"I don't know what you mean."

I quickened my steps to keep up with his long strides. My stomach clenched with fear and my dragon begged to be released—my magic burning in my veins.

Axel pulled me into a room guarded by two Shadow dragons. He dropped my arm and closed the door behind us. When he turned and looked at me, dark magic swirled around his eyes. His white flames spiraled down his arms and lashed out chaotically. He stormed toward me and I backed against the opposite wall, ready to strike out.

He wrapped his hand around my throat with the lightest of pressures. I waited, not wanting to reveal myself until absolutely necessary. White flames burned away the dark magic in his eyes and he whispered in my ear.

"Don't lie to me, Zale. I know about Julie."

My heart stopped. "Don't hurt her. Please. It was me."

He dropped his hand and backed up.

"I'm not going to hurt her."

I furrowed my brow and swallowed. The place where his fingers touched my neck still burned hot. I pushed off the wall and righted myself.

"What are you going to do?"

A grin spread across his face and he began to unbutton his shirt. I turned my gaze away, unsure what he was planning.

Axel walked slowly to me and reached out to touch my cheek. He tilted my face so he could look at my eyes. "I want you to take the Shadows from me."

"What?"

"Will you free me, princess?"

Chapter Thirty-Two

Zale

"Free you? You want me to take the Shadows *from* you?"

He nodded and stepped back, continuing to unbutton his shirt.

"Why? I don't understand. You *are* the Shadows."

He shook his head. "If you start working, I promise to tell you my story."

"Now?"

His eyes locked with mine. "I've been waiting a long time for you, Zale."

The use of my name shocked me out of my stillness. I stood in front of him and put my hands on his chest, searching out the Shadows. What other opportunity would I get to rid the Dragon King of the Shadows? They shot out of him and struck at my hands, resisting me. I recoiled at the sting.

"They...have never done that before."

"The Shadows are deep. I do not expect you to be able to do it all at once."

I put my hands on his chest again and concentrated, pulling slower than before. The Shadows rose out of him and twisted around my arms but didn't strike me. It would have to be a slow draw, like pulling poison from blood instead of ripping out a knife or sword.

Axel closed his eyes and let out a breath, his chest rising and falling under my fingers.

"You did not create the Shadows? You don't want them?"

Axel put his hands over mine, holding them in place on his chest. "No."

"Then how? How are you filled with them? Why can't you be rid of them?"

He shook his head. "I don't know everything. The Shadows hide parts of my memories and twist others."

I focused my concentration on the dark magic, eager to free him and ignoring what this could mean for dragons everywhere. That would have to wait for now. "What do you know?"

"I know that you saved me once already. I know you will do it again."

I met his eyes as my magic pulled on the Shadows. "Saved you?"

"When you cut the cord, the pain opened my eyes to the truth. I held onto that pain and it guides me. Keeps my mind sharp."

My fingers twitched and I looked down, uncomfortable with this new information.

"I...wouldn't have done it if I had known you were..."

"Manipulated?"

I nodded. "I didn't know."

Axel squeezed my hand on his chest. "I know. *I* didn't know. I still don't know how long it has been since Celeste found me."

"The witch? She is the one who created the dark magic?"

He nodded. "Yes. I still don't know how she found me. I cut my cords so I wouldn't be found."

I pulled on the Shadows, and he hissed. "I'm sorry."

"Don't. This is going to hurt a lot more than that. I know it's been decades, perhaps a century or two."

"A century?" My heart ached at the thought of any dragon being under the influence of the Shadows for that long.

"How did she do it? Maybe we can stop her if we knew..."

"I don't know. I can't even remember her plan exactly. I've been trying to get her to tell me again since you cut the cord, but she is tricky."

A sudden thought crossed my mind, and I lifted my hands from his chest. What if he were trying to deceive me? To find out the source of my powers or some other nefarious plan.

He took my hands and placed them back on his chest. "I've known about your powers for some time. Why would I want you to take the Shadows from me if I were working with the witch?"

"How did you..." *How did he know my thoughts?*

His silver eyes turned molten and my breath hitched in my chest. "I may no longer have a cord connecting you to me, but that doesn't mean that I am no longer your soulmate."

"It doesn't?"

"No. Not to me."

I concentrated on my hands and pulled more of the Shadows from his body, the task far easier than considering he might be telling me the truth.

"Does it matter to you?"

His voice held the smallest bit of vulnerability and I wanted to tell him that of course it didn't matter to give him some comfort, but it would be a lie. I wasn't sure. What if this were some ruse?

I had others to think about. I couldn't only think about my own wants and needs, even if I knew what exactly they were. I might not be leading, but I was still a queen.

"I don't know."

He gently squeezed my hand again. "I will earn your trust. Give me time."

I raised my eyes to his. "Time is something we are lacking, Axel. Especially if what you are telling me is true. We don't know what the witch's timeline is."

I returned my concentration back to the Shadows and pulled them out bit by bit.

"When Celeste comes looking for you, I want you here."

"Here? Aren't these your rooms?"

"They are."

"Axel, that will be suspicious. Return me to the prison."

"I can't protect—"

I flashed my flames down my arms and my gold tattoos lifted on my skin. My dragon flared to life beneath my skin.

"I can protect myself."

"But..."

"It is my choice. My choice when to use my magic, when to allow my dragon to rise."

He put his hands on my face, turning my eyes to his. "Don't hold back. Use it."

"I want to free as many as I can before that is discovered."

A small smile crossed his face as he stroked his thumbs over my cheeks. The gesture sent shivers over my body. "You are a queen worthy of them."

I opened my mouth to respond but a knock sounded at the door. I dropped my hands and Axel buttoned up his shirt. He guided me to a seat on the other side of the room and then positioned himself near his desk.

Celeste entered a moment later and my hatred for her burned hotter than before. She was using him. Exploiting him.

"What is she doing here?"

"I had questions for her." Axel's tone returned to the arrogance it had before we were alone.

"And you couldn't wait for me?" Celeste placed her hand delicately on her hip.

He waved his hand in the air, dismissing both of us. "She won't say anything anyway. Have her escorted back to the prison."

"I'll take her myself, Your Majesty." Celeste crossed the room and dug her fingers into my arm harder than necessary. "Come on, High Queen. Let's get you back to your *room*."

I followed her out to the hall, not daring to lift my eyes to see Axel.

She gripped me with fury all the way to the bars of my cell. As she pulled the door shut, she paused and tilted her head. Her brow raised and a small frown formed on her lips. "Did the Dragon King ask anything of you, High Queen?"

I sat on my stone cot, hoping that nothing in my movements betrayed me.

"No. Nothing at all."

Chapter Thirty-Three

Zale

"Here. He wanted me to bring you more water."

"Julie. Stop. Don't come down here again today."

"I won't stop. You need it. You need your strength."

I shook my head and turned away from the bars of my cell. "The only way I am able to keep doing this is to stay secret."

"It won't matter if you get enough—"

I turned and my tattoos flashed on my skin. I was frustrated and tired of hiding. Her words did not ease my agitation. "I won't get enough if you blow my cover. Hidden in a prison in the heart of enemy territory is a perfect place for me. But I have to move slow. And this is not slow."

Julie dipped her head, her brunette hair sliding around her face.

"Tell him to find out what her plan is. I will continue with my work."

I faced the back of my cell again and listened to her footsteps retreat from the prison. Her hope was almost contagious, but I knew better. I'd been pulling Shadows out of dragons for years. They didn't want to let go of their hosts. There had to be hundreds if not thousands of dragons here in Shadowkeep. It would take me decades to free them all.

"Her plan...is to...unite them all."

I walked to the bars and leaned my head against them. "I know, Marcos. I...don't know how."

"With the sword."

"The sword?"

The chains around him rattled and echoed off the stone as he turned and sat on his cot. "There is a sword that can unite the Heart of the Sea and the Heart of the Mountain. Or so the legends say."

I searched the recesses of my mind—all the prophecies my dreams had shown me, all the words that Keani had shared. Only the one Keani wrote in blood mentioned a sword. I rolled the words over in my mind, trying to fit them in the pieces of what I knew.

Oceans are frozen deep

Remember the tides

Mountains will crumble

Fires will rise

Hiding in silence

The Shadows are alive

All roads point to this time

Use the sword to survive

The King is coming

His time has arrived

The sword to survive. So I had been right all along. Uniting the clans was the answer to freeing the dragons from the Shadows.

And the king is coming? Did that foresee that I would free him from the Shadows? There was still a long process between me and that end. Especially when we only had moments at a time together.

Wander.

The voice in my mind echoed again and I winced. The voice was stronger than before. It always came at the worst times. My body begged to find the sea, but even if I wanted to, the bars held me here.

I pushed away the voice. There were other problems to solve. Where was this sword? Could it unite the Hearts?

Wander.

The voice pressed in on my mind, distracting me from my thoughts. Why was it here? It left when my dragon didn't acknowledge me. Why was it back now?

Visions of white landscapes with greens and blues and yellows flashing around the sky bombarded my mind.

Wander.

"Go away."

"Tiamat?"

Wander.

"Go away! I can not wander even if I wanted to!"

"High Queen?"

The voice fled my mind and Marcos's concern brought me back to the present. "I...I am all right."

"Who were you talking to?"

"It doesn't matter."

"There is nothing but time here, Tiamat. Tell me. Maybe I can help."

I sat on the cot and ran my hands through my hair, pulling it off my neck. "There is a voice. It called to me before, and it calls to me now."

"A voice? In your head?"

I scoffed. "I know how it sounds."

After several moments of silence, Marcos spoke again. "There are many magics in this world, Tiamat. How do you know it is not one of them?"

"I don't know what it is. I have never been able to follow it."

The door at the end of the hall slammed against the stone wall, and I expected to see Axel coming to chastise me for something.

Instead, Celeste prowled down the hall. Her black dress and the Shadows intertwined in a pool around her feet and rivers of ash behind her. In her hand, she held a solid black dagger with jagged edges. She stopped in front of my cell and placed her hand on her hip.

"I know you don't want to share the stone, but I think I found a way to take it from you."

I clasped my hands together at my waist and lifted my chin, ready to face her.

Celeste waved her hand and the Shadows moved the door out of her way. I held my ground, waiting for her to approach. She stopped inches from my face. Her lips twisted into a wicked grin and she patted my cheek. "Hold still for me, will you?"

I turned my head away from her hand, but the Shadows encircled my waist, my ankles, my wrists, throwing me against the stone wall. I took a breath and braced myself for the onslaught again.

"This should do the trick." Celeste lifted the dagger up to examine it and ran her tongue along the edge.

"What is it?"

"Shadows." She raised the dagger and tried to cut my chest where the stone resided.

"This won't work."

"We'll see." She pressed the blade to my skin and the dark magic burned me with its icy touch. She dug the blade into my chest and I screamed.

Agony was the only word to use for the way the Shadows split into my chest and reached for my soul. I called my dragon, and she pushed back against the Shadows. My gold tattoos lifted on my skin and blue flames spiraled around me.

Celeste's grin moved to a snarl. She cut my skin over the stone and pulled it back to where it rested over my heart. The deep blues of the Heart of the Sea pulsed around me and fought to stitch my skin back together.

With blue fire surrounding her hand, she grasped the stone and wrapped her fingers around it. Tears leaked from my eyes as I fought the Shadows. They slid into my mind and wrestled with my dragon for control.

"Give up, High Queen. No one can resist them for long."

"No!"

Celeste pulled on the Heart of the Sea and a deep blue flame rose out of me. The stone burned and threw Celeste across the cell, knocking her into the bars.

With her blade no longer on my skin, I flushed the Shadows from my body. My tattoos settled into me and I held my hands over the stone, breathing heavily. The muscles and skin stitched themselves back together to hold the Heart of the Sea in place.

Celeste rose to her feet and released a groan. She picked up her blade and held it outstretched toward me.

"This isn't over!"

She spun and locked the cell behind herself, storming out of the prison.

Chapter Thirty-Four

Zale

I would take the torture over this silence.

No one came.

It had to be days.

At least in the torture, there was no wondering. No time to pause and consider how I found myself here.

Marcos's breathing became more irregular, his moans more infrequent.

Where was Julie?

Where was Axel?

Celeste?

What was happening in the keep?

I paced the cell for the thousandth time, only my memories and the voice to keep me company.

Wander.

I squeezed my eyes shut, blocking it out.

My soul stirred like troubled waters, and I unwrapped the wounds I carried for too long without tending to them. I sat on the stone cot and pulled my knees up to my chest. Tears fell down my face before I had allowed them.

I wondered what would have happened if I had saved Nyla from the Shadows. How long had she had them? Did she suffer for long?

I couldn't find it in myself to be angry with her. Her actions cut me so deep, but it wasn't her fault. She loved me. She always had.

Would I have that again? Someone to trust so completely. Someone who I knew like my own reflection?

I sobbed when I saw Lance in my mind. He had been my safety—a calm to the storm I held inside me. Would anyone ever settle me the way he did? Would anyone ever know me so deeply?

Would there be anyone to hold my secrets again?

Wander.

I rose and wiped the tears away. "Marcos?"

No answer. I listened and his breathing was hardly more than a whisper of breath.

"Marcos! Please answer me."

The chains rattled and I breathed a sigh of relief. He had at least moved.

"Marcos, if you can hear me, please don't leave yet. Keep fighting. I'm going to save you."

"Save...it...for...someone...else."

I wrapped my hands around the bars.

"No. Keep fighting. There are so many that I can't save. You won't be one of them."

Anger rose inside me and my gold tattoos surfaced. "I can't lose another friend."

My flames flashed around me and I struggled to contain them.

The door at the end of the hall slapped the stone wall with a bang. "Tiamat!" Three dragons carried something between them. Some*one*.

"Tiamat. Help!"

My entire world slowed down and even my breathing stopped. Between the three dragons on a sheet lay Axel—his jaw slack and blood staining his shirt and the sheet. So much blood.

I shot flames into the door of my cell and sent it flying off its hinges—the time for secrecy long gone–my power spurred on by my frustration and fear.

"What happened?"

"I don't know," Julie panted as they set him on the stone floor. "I found him like this. He's lucky it was me and not someone else."

I ripped his shirt down the front and put my hands on his chest, blood pooling beneath my fingers. The Shadows were stronger than before when I pulled them from him.

"Find me water. Hurry!" One of the dragons ran down the hall to follow my instructions.

My fingers traced the edge of the wound, encouraging it to heal. The Shadows pulled it open again and again. I poured what little water I had from inside me into the wound, begging the sea to heal him.

Axel's eyes opened and flared white with his flames. "Celeste...the dagger...Shadows...still inside..."

I plunged my finger into the wound, feeling for the sharp edge. His heart beat against my finger and the sharp edge was lodged at the very edge.

I closed my eyes.

No.

I needed the sea. I needed more water than they could ever bring me.

"What is it?" Julie asked.

"The tip of the dagger is lodged next to his heart. I need to get him to the ocean."

"We're leagues and leagues from the sea, Tiamat. There's no way he will survive that long."

Chains rattled in the cell next to us. "Portal."

I let out a breath. Of course. Marcos was from Mountain clan. "Can you make us one?"

Marcos nodded. I glanced at Axel before I stood and destroyed the bars of his cell. One of the dragons returned with water and I poured it on Marcos's skin as I laid my hand on my friend. I pulled on the Shadows. His brown eyes filled with fire, and he fought them with me. I drew them out of him and he pushed them away. They dissipated above our heads in a cloud of smoke.

His breathing grew stronger and as I pulled the last of them from his veins, he rose to his feet. He looked over his hands and purple flames spiraled around his arms and chest as he grinned.

"Free...I didn't dare to hope."

I couldn't help but to smile back at the joy on his face. "Hello, my friend."

Marcos wrapped his arms around me and lifted me off my feet. "Thank you." He set me down and bowed deeply. "High Queen."

"Can you help me get him to the sea?"

"Are you sure? Wouldn't it be better to let him die? Escape and rally dragons to you?"

I looked back at Axel, bleeding and barely conscious on the stone. "My instinct is to save him. He doesn't want the Shadows. If I can free him, he will be helpful to us."

Marcos nodded. "I will trust you, Tiamat."

He walked to the back of his cell, the motions even and fluid with his renewed strength. He lifted his hands above his head and his flames spiraled from his chest to his fingertips. He traced the pattern of a doorway into the air, leaving flames following the path. When the door was finished, he put his hand in the center, and it disappeared from view. He grinned. "Looks like I still have the touch."

Julie picked up one end of the makeshift hammock. "Who else is from Mountain clan?"

The other two dragons shook their heads. She glanced to Marcos. "It's just you and me then."

"I've never traveled by portal before."

He took my hand. "You'll need to touch me so you can use it. You two, hold onto Julie's shoulders as she walks."

"What about Axel?"

"He's rogue, right?"

I nodded.

"He will be uncomfortable, but he will be able to pass through."

Marcos took hold of the other end of the makeshift hammock. "Come. There's no time to rest."

I glanced around the cell and for a brief moment, my heart ached for those I was leaving behind, here, but there was no more time.

"Tiamat?"

I nodded and tightened my grip on his hand. "Let's go. Take me as close to the sea as you can."

Marcos passed into the portal, and I followed behind with my flames spiraling around me, ready for whatever lay on the other side.

Chapter Thirty-Five

Zale

Nausea rose quickly as I entered the portal. I stumbled, but Marcos steadied me. The foreign magic pushed on me and tried to split me in two. I never had to use the portals before. The sea carried me wherever I needed to travel.

"What is this? Marcos...it's tearing me apart."

"Hold onto me, Tiamat. We don't have far to go."

A hand wrapped around my free wrist. Silver eyes stared wildly into mine. Axel wrapped white flames around my arms and my chest. They hovered over my body, protecting me from the foreign magic. The pressure lifted and I quickened my steps behind Marcos.

"Come, Tiamat. See? That light there? It's your sea."

I focused on the end of the tunnel, each step growing heavier.

Wander.

Why? Why was the voice here in this portal?

Wander.

The light grew and with a sudden burst, I stepped out onto cold, wet sand gasping for air. Axel's white flames faded and he released my wrist. Marcos and Julie dropped the hammock that carried Axel and the two Sea dragons coughed and choked as they caught their breath.

"Hurry. She may not be far behind." I pointed to the portal.

Marcos grabbed the corner of the portal and pulled it down, his flames sealing the space.

I straightened and let the salty wind whip around my face, welcoming the sea but not quite believing I was here. For the first time in what felt like a lifetime, I was home.

The sun began to set on the horizon and my sea spread out in every direction. I stepped forward and my dragon sprang to life beneath my skin, begging to be released. With my tattoos and fire flaring out of me, I picked up speed, running into the waves. I dove beneath the surface, shifting.

My dragon stretched and arched her neck like a cat. I whipped my tail and spread my wings under the surface, feeling every muscle and scale and bit of strength in this form. It had been too long since I was in this form. Too long without the grace and power that my dragon held.

I soaked in the water, the salt, and the stone hummed in my chest, happy to be reunited with the sea. My body filled out and healed in all the little ways and contented joy filled my soul. There was nothing quite like the sea. Nothing that could compare with her comfort.

When my lungs began to burn, I pulled my dragon back inside as I shifted. We had work to do, and it would not be easy.

I kicked my legs to the surface and pulled in air when I broke through. Pushing my hair back in place, I waded to the beach. My steps were sure and steady for the first time since I cut the cord.

I patted Marcos's shoulder. "Rest my friend. You did well."

Turning to the Sea dragons, I motioned for them to pick up the sheet that held the Dragon King. "I need your help to get him into the sea. What are your names?"

The two males grabbed the sheet and lifted Axel, who groaned as they moved him. We needed to hurry. His skin was far too pale from the blood he had lost.

"Ramos."

"Tamil."

"Ramos, Tamil. Thank you. We need to get him into the water, past the waves. Can you do it?"

They nodded and I followed them, stilling the water as much as I was able. When we were up to our chests and past the waves, I instructed them to stretch the sheet taut, allowing Axel to float but still be connected to the water.

I placed my hands on his chest and felt the wound again, my fingers searching for the metal. He groaned and his eyes opened.

"Gentle...princess...that's my heart."

"This is going to hurt." I brought my flames up to my fingers and water collected under my hands. I looked at him for a moment, compassion flooding my heart for this dragon. "Don't die."

Before he could respond, I used the water to begin moving the shard from the blade away from his heart. The Shadows fought against me, tugging and pushing to keep the metal where it was. I pulled them away and let them hiss into the air above us.

The blade tip began to move, and Axel groaned. By feel, I navigated the metal out of his heart. I guided it out with the sea through the entrance of his wound. The water lifted the dark metal to me, and I held it in my palm. With one hand on Axel's chest and the other with the black dagger tip, I examined the dark magic. It hummed with a life of its own.

"It's alive...or it's that concentrated?"

"Destroy it. With fire."

Axel was right. It was fascinating that Celeste could concentrate the dark magic so strongly into the metal but it was dangerous. Witches had many ways to manipulate magic. It was best to destroy this. I let my flames consume the dagger tip and washed my palm clean with the sea.

The Shadows inside Axel continued to fight me as I pulled more out of him. I used the sea to seal his wound. His eyes met mine and he reached for my cheek. Before his hand met my skin, his face contorted in pain and he groaned.

Shadows spiraled around him and cut at my hands.

He needed rest before I pulled more Shadows from him. We all needed rest.

"Let's get him out of the water. We need to find shelter."

Ramos, Tamil, and I waded back through the waves to the beach. Julie waited for us with Marcos.

"There are some caves down the beach, Tiamat. We should be able to rest there until we can find something better."

"Caves are good. Until I know more about this war and what has happened since I was imprisoned, we need to remain hidden."

We followed her to the caves and Marcos set up a fire with driftwood to ward off the cold. We were somewhere in the north. Likely the northwestern Canadian shores if my memories were correct.

Ramos and Tamil laid the sheet down on the sand and Axel groaned softly before settling his head to the side.

We gathered around the fire, staring out over the ocean. It was strange to be anywhere beside the prison of Shadowkeep. I wasn't sure I would ever be free.

"What now, Tiamat? What are you going to do next?"

I glanced back at Axel and then to my new companions—each of them looking to me to lead.

"Rest. And plan. And heal."

Chapter Thirty-Six

Zale

I traced my fingers in the sand, the ocean reaching up to dance with my hand, both of us relieved to be close to the other. My skin soaked in the healing waters every time the waves reached me.

"The Shadows attacked most of the major players. I know the Order was training militaries all over the world," Julie said.

"Celeste ordered a retaliation on the headquarters where we believe the Order is," Ramos offered.

"Do you know where it is?"

Each of them shook their heads.

"I've been imprisoned for decades, if what you're telling me is true. It's still hard for me to wrap my head around." Marcos shifted uncomfortably.

I nodded my head. "Desmond died and Sybil became regent almost thirty years ago. It was...upsetting to the politics between the clans."

"I was there when he died. I remember when the Dragon King found us. To this day, I still do not understand why he did not kill me. I suppose I should be thankful for the Shadows in that way." He tossed a stick into the flames of the fire. "What of the Mountain Queen? You said he had a child."

"She...fell. I don't know who leads the Mountain dragons now."

"What about Sea clan? Surely, they still stand?" Marcos's eyes met mine with hope.

I looked out over the sea. "What is left of my clan is scattered. I feel their magic flowing through me, but in every direction. It would take time to call them together. We need to rest, Marcos. Not every problem will have a solution tonight."

Ramos stood and stoked the fire. "I'll take the first watch. Rest, High Queen."

I inclined my head to him. In a cave with four dragons and a dragon king enslaved to the Shadows was not how I saw my future, but it was what I had now, and I would make the best of it. It was better than being locked in the prison of Shadowkeep.

I laid on my side, watching Axel. His chest rose and fell slowly, his shirt covered in his blood. The Shadows still rested in him. Could we trust him? I sat upright and Julie caught my eye. She looked at Axel and back to me.

"I will take the first watch with the Dragon King, Tiamat."

I nodded. Tomorrow, I would not stop until the Shadows were gone from him. I did not trust that we were hidden from Celeste until he was free.

When I awoke and the first rays of the sun hit my face, the first thing I noticed was the sheet was empty. I sat upright and glanced around the cave. Julie held her finger to her lips, and I rose to join her at the cave's entrance.

Down the beach, Axel sat with his hands on his knees, staring over the water.

"How long has he been awake?" I whispered.

"About an hour."

"And did he say anything?"

"No, he has been sitting there, watching the waves as the sun rises."

I brushed the sand off my arm and side. "Thank you, Julie."

My feet relished in the feel of the sand as I walked toward him. Each step healed a piece of my fractured heart. He turned his head when I was close.

"I forgot how beautiful the sea is in the morning."

I looked out over the waves and smiled. "She is always beautiful."

When he didn't respond, I glanced back to find him staring. His observation of me sent waves of heat through my body but I brushed them aside. I licked my lips and clasped my hands in front of myself, ready to face this day.

He rose and took several steps closer.

"I would tell you that the sea could not rival your beauty, princess, but you're not ready to hear it. I would tell you—"

I put my hand on his chest. "You're right. I am not ready to hear that from you." I stepped back and met his eyes, my hand dropping back to my side. "I need to purge the Shadows from you. Today."

Axel's silver eyes turned molten, and I wanted to let him tell me the things he would say, but I could not allow the sentiment. That was all it was anyway. A nice sentiment. A soulmate who was no longer a soulmate, who wanted that connection.

"What do you need from me, Zale?"

I took a breath. "Go out into the waves. I will speak with Julie and Marcos then join you."

He nodded and waded into the ocean without another word.

Julie and Marcos joined me on the beach when I motioned them closer. "I need protection. My full concentration needs to be on removing the Shadows. Can you relieve Ramos and Tamil? I don't know how long this will take."

"Whatever you need, Tiamat."

I twisted my hair back away from my face, the unruly curls fighting the restraint, and waded into the ocean. When I was a couple steps from Axel, I met his eyes for a brief moment. The intensity with which he looked at me was unsettling. I let my blue flames spiral around me and hit the surface of the ocean. The droplets hovered around us in the old script. The words didn't make sense.

Dark.

Hide.

Bind.

Blood.

Lost.

Axel looked over the droplets. "I know these words."

"Do they mean something to you?"

His brows furrowed and he shook his head. "Maybe once upon a time."

I stepped up to him and pulled his shirt off his chest, letting it flow away. I put my hand against his skin and let my other hand send fog to surround us. When it was no one but he and I and the sea, I searched out the Shadows.

The dark magic lashed out fiercely from his chest, tightening its grip on my arm and sliding up to my neck. Axel reached his hand out to pull the Shadows back.

"Don't. You have to fight them. Not protect me."

"Zale."

"This is how we defeat them. You fight them. I fight them."

He lifted his eyes and stared over my head before nodding. White flames flashed in his eyes and I smiled. Deep blue from the Heart of the Sea joined my fire as I searched through his body for the Shadows.

I drained them from his veins and the chambers of his heart. I swept them from his lungs and searched them out from his throat.

When that was done, I entered his mind, placing my hands on either side of his head. The Shadows lurked in every space, in every memory. I burned away where they built their home. I shone light where they tried to hide and escape my notice.

The sea flowed in me and rejuvenated me every time I lost strength. The dark magic slipped away into the air, hissing out of existence. The fog around us blocked out everything, including the sun, leaving us in a dark blue igloo of flames.

Axel pushed and I pulled, until the last of the Shadows left his body. A shriek filled the air and the words in the old script shimmered. Magic shook inside me, not responding to the normal order of our world. This was more than just Shadows.

The dark magic rushed back down and dove into Axel's chest, leaving a burn in a symbol on his skin. A symbol I had seen before.

A circle with lines through it like the sun.

It was the same hex Celeste used on Maddie.

I grinned. I broke the hex once before. I would do it again.

Were those her screams that filled the air? I certainly hoped so.

Axel breathed heavily. "It's too much, princess."

"Let me worry about that."

I called to the sea. She rose around me and opened my chest, letting the Heart of the Sea escape. I held the stone in my hand and pressed it against Axel's skin. My flames mixed with those of the stone, and I stripped him of the Shadows again.

In a flash that shot straight up to the heavens, the Heart of the Sea broke through the hex. The shriek died as the last of the Shadows evaporated in the air.

I grinned and let the fog of my magic slip away.

Axel stood before me, free of the Shadows.

Chapter Thirty-Seven

Zale

I placed the Heart of the Sea against my chest and the stone buried itself under my skin once more.

Axel breathed out slowly and shouted at the sky. He laughed and the sound sang to my heart like music. He wrapped his arms around me and lifted me, spinning me in the waves. I placed my hands on his shoulders, letting him enjoy the moment.

He let me slide down his body and my hands rested on his chest.

"Thank you, Princess. That's three times you have saved me now."

I offered him a slight smile. "Maybe you will have the chance to return the favor."

He placed his hand on my cheek. "I hope I never have to. I want your life to always be safe."

"My life will not always be safe. I am High Queen of Sea clan. And we are at war."

His eyes darkened and he dropped his hand back to his side. "Yes. We are."

It was easy to turn away from him. Without the Shadows, Axel was different. He was vibrant, full of life. How much of his memory had returned? Would they all come back to him? Would it take time? I didn't miss the way his eyes began to assess our situation—his mind quickly moving from joy to strategy.

I should have expected no different from the Dragon King.

We waded out of the water and my steps betrayed me. I stumbled and Axel caught me around the waist. He pulled me into his side and supported my weight.

"I need to rest."

"I would say so." He put his hands behind my knees and lifted me with ease. I placed my hand against his chest.

"Axel, this isn't necessary. I can walk."

He said nothing as he carried me to the cave and set me down on the warm sand by the fire. His smell intoxicated me, and I fought against my desire to rest my head against his chest.

Julie handed me some fish that she had caught earlier, breaking my thoughts.

"Eat. You need your strength."

Wander.

The voice echoed around the cave and tugged on my heart. I pulled my legs beneath myself, attempting to rise. I whispered before I had a chance to realize the words held no meaning for the others. "Do you hear that?"

"The voice?"

My eyes whipped to Axel's. "You heard it?"

He nodded. Moving to my side, he crouched and gently pressed on my shoulder. "Rest, princess. We will chase down the voice another day."

Wander.

I sucked in a breath, the pull of the sea and the voice threatening to break me apart.

"Zale."

I tilted my chin to look at him. His face wrinkled in concern.

Wander.

I winced. I needed to go.

"Let me hold you."

"No. I have to go."

"I hear it too, princess. We don't need you stumbling through the ocean and sand in this state to get to it."

"It's...not always this intense."

"Then, let me hold you. Let me anchor you here. It's the least I can offer you."

"Axel..."

Wander.

His silver eyes darkened. "Zale."

"All right." I nodded. What harm could it do? He was free of the Shadows and maybe it would bring me some comfort.

Axel settled himself against the wall of the cave and opened his arms, letting me come to him on my own.

I leaned against him, my back tucked against his side, my ear against his chest. I didn't think about how good it felt to have him wrap his arms around me and draw me closer. I didn't think about the dragons looking on. I let myself drift, wondering if I would sleep or I would go to the in-between.

My eyes opened slowly as the light drifted across the cave.

So it had been sleep. Not the in-between.

I began to lift my head and arms tightened around me. A flush spread over me as I remembered I was still in Axel's arms. I laid my head back on his chest, listening to the rise and fall of his breath, savoring the feel of him.

But it was too good to be true. It had to be.

I cleared my throat and his breathing changed as he woke. He ran his hand down my arm, chills followed his touch. I pushed away from him and sat up, our eyes locking as I did.

He reached his hand up and tucked my hair behind my ear. "Good morning, princess."

I swallowed and wished for words. Any words. But the intensity of his gaze froze me in place. My heart beat rapidly in my chest and my breathing stilled.

"I haven't slept so well in centuries." His eyes darted all over my face as he spoke, looking for a response.

I waited for my body to finally respond to my will. There was no answer for that. At least, no answer that would bring either of us joy. I pushed myself up to my feet and walked out of the cave to the beach, leaving his words hanging in the air.

The waves crashed on the sand, and I knew the moment that Axel stood at my side, my body attuned with his presence. Was that what it was like to have a soulmate? Or was it the irresistible attraction that I held for him?

Either way, I pushed the sensations aside.

"What did the witch do to you, Axel?"

"She was after the Heart of the Sea. I know that much."

"Clearly she didn't get it."

He shook his head. "No. The only thing she said was that she didn't need me any longer. I wasn't expecting such a direct attack."

"She left you to bleed out? You owe Julie your life. Ramos and Tamil too."

"You saved me."

"Only because they brought you to me. I was in the prison, remember?"

"Hmm. I only remember you." He scanned the skies. "We should move. It's not good for us to stay in one place."

"I couldn't agree more." I turned and marched to the cave.

"Do you have a place in mind?"

"I do."

"Care to share?"

I gave him a quick glance. "An island. Medney island to be exact."

There was still one rogue alive that I trusted completely. At least, he was alive when I last saw him. And I needed to have all the help I could get to take down the Shadows.

Chapter Thirty-Eight

Zale

"We should stay together," Marcos argued.

"I need to travel to an island. I'll be traveling in the ocean."

"I can make a portal there."

I shook my head. "Do you remember the rogue? Simeon?"

"That no-good selfish dragon—"

"Is the closest thing to family I have left. And I need him."

Marcos snapped his mouth shut. He glanced at Axel and then back to me. "You are full of surprises, Tiamat. I still don't like this plan."

"He is free of the Shadows, Marcos. As are you. If he means me harm, Simeon is the best match we have remaining." My heart squeezed and I couldn't help but to think of Jenna.

"You underestimate yourself, Tiamat."

"I understand the limits of my powers. Can I trust you with your task?"

Marcos nodded. "We will look for the Mountain dragons. But how will I reach you when we do?"

"Simeon can take me to you."

"That's unsettling, Tiamat."

I grinned. "You should be unsettled." I laid my hands on his shoulders. "Thank you, my dear friend. I would not have survived that prison cell without you."

Marcos bowed low. "High Queen, it was an honor. I look forward to seeing you again."

"The honor was mine, Mountain warrior."

He glanced at Axel and then nodded before heading down the beach with Julie.

"We will see them again." Axel's words were welcomed, and I nodded.

"Yes. We will." I turned and faced Tamil and Ramos. "You will need to stay close to me, and stay in the sea until I can speak with Simeon. I'm sure Medney is set with many traps."

I turned to face Axel and he held his hand up. "Don't bother telling me not to come. I am more than capable of handling my own affairs."

"As you see fit." When I turned to face the sea, I grinned. He must underestimate Simeon, which is why Simeon had remained the most dangerous dragon I knew to date.

We entered the waves and one by one we shifted. I led the way through the icy waters, my wings pressed close to my side as we slid through the ocean. I found the currents and all manner of sea creatures escaped my path as we traveled.

It was easy to feel the border of Simeon's territory. The stones he gathered over centuries held his magic and created a thickness in the sea and air. I motioned to Tamil and Ramos to circle back to the sea. I would call them after assessing the situation.

Axel and I shifted in the waves. A small figure with dark hair stood on the beach, waiting for us.

I scanned the air, looking for Simeon. He wouldn't leave his soulmate.

Samara raced down the beach toward us, white and orange flames spiraling down her arms.

"Wait! Samara! Wait!"

She pushed her flames into Axel and sent him tumbling down the beach. She ignored me and continued to fire on Axel.

"Samara! He is free of the Shadows."

She kicked his chest as he rose and sent more flames into him. A latticework of white flames erupted around Axel, holding him in place.

I drew from the sea and released smoke, trapping her in the center with me. She spun, her flames still hot around her arms. "You brought him here! He tried to kill me! He tried to kill Simeon!"

"He was under the influence of the Shadows."

Samara sent white fire at my head, and I deflected it.

"He tortured me! He tortured *him*!"

I pulled water from the ocean and dumped it on her head. Her flames dissipated. "I pulled the Shadows from him myself, Samara. It is not what you think."

She coughed and lifted her hair from her face. Her scowl seared my soul. I needed her trust. I needed her help.

"You better have a really good reason for being here, Zale. Simeon won't wake—"

"What? He still sleeps?"

"Yes. For many weeks. Ever since the Dragon King struck him."

I lifted my fog and Axel stood with blood running down his face and white flames dangerously in his palm. The latticework of the trap was no longer visible. I stormed to him and put my finger on his chest. "What did you do to Simeon?"

He glanced over my shoulder at Samara and then back to me. "I can reverse it. It was...a safety measure."

"I don't believe him," Samara shouted down the beach.

"If you can reverse it, why do it in the first place?"

His eyes darted between mine. "I...Zale, can we talk about this after?"

I narrowed my eyes on him. "No. You can tell me now."

"I need Simeon. I need him alive."

"Why?"

Axel put his hands on my shoulders. "I know I haven't earned it yet, but please can you trust me?"

"I do not trust you." Rage thrummed in my body, but I worked to cool it. A little bit of trust could be given. "But if you can save him, I will try to."

"Zale—" Samara stepped closer, and her flames hovered in her hands.

"Let him, Samara. If he tries anything, I will kill him myself."

She chewed on her lip and finally nodded once before turning and heading up the slope toward the cottage. Axel put his hand on my lower back as we walked. I allowed the intimacy despite my conflicting emotions. Perhaps he would be able to save Simeon. Perhaps he was telling the truth.

Chapter Thirty-Nine

Zale

S amara pushed the door to the cottage open and it slapped against the wall with a bang.

"We have company," she said as she pushed her way across the room to a closed door.

Maddie and Jesse rose from the couch. Maddie's rounded belly was so large, it appeared she would be due anytime now. Jesse tugged her behind himself and watched as we entered.

Their eyes locked on Axel behind me.

"Axel."

"Jesse."

I glanced between the two, each assessing the other. It was strange to remember that the two had a different kind of past from when Axel was hiding in the Order.

"This way. Unless you want me to kill you for wasting time? I'm not feeling very patient." Samara held open a door and soft lighting filled the room. I followed Axel inside and sucked in a breath.

Simeon lay on the bed, perfectly still. The ridges of his face were more prominent, and he was so pale.

"Is he alive?" I whispered.

"The fact that I'm standing here is proof he is. But he hasn't moved since Axel struck him." Samara leveled a glare at Axel. "If you harm him, my dying breath will be used to kill you."

Axel nodded and moved to the side of Simeon's bed. He hovered his hands over Simeon's chest and sent a bolt of white flames into his body.

Simeon's eyes opened and he gasped for air. He scanned the room and sent white flames into Axel's chest, throwing him against the wall.

"You bastard!" Simeon sat up on the edge of the bed and Samara moved to his side. "Why the hell did you think it was okay to put me in a coma?"

"It was for your safety."

"I don't need to be kept safe," he growled. "I'm rogue."

Axel straightened and ran his hand down his shirt. "You did. I needed Celeste to believe that you and the Mountain Queen are dead."

I stepped closer to Axel. "Why?"

"Because the only way to truly unite the clan's magic is through the power of the rogues."

Silence settled on the room.

"Unite them?" Samara asked.

"How do you think we will defeat the Shadow magic?"

"It appeared we lost..."

Axel glanced at me. "This war is not over. Celeste wanted to unite the clans and bind them to the Shadows, effectively making her ruler of all dragons. She would need the rogues for this. But now? You, High Queen, have changed the tides."

"We will see." I turned and left the small room. Jesse still stood in front of Maddie, watching everything. Her eyes were round, and she held her abdomen.

"You look well, Maddie."

"Zale...what is going on?" Her voice trembled as she spoke. "What is Axel doing here?"

I glanced over my shoulder. "You'll have to ask him for yourself."

Jesse put his hand on my arm. "Zale. Are we safe? I can't have—"

"You are as safe as you are around Simeon or me. He is still a dragon."

"We were comrades once, Jesse," Axel appeared at my shoulder.

"You were hiding as a dragon. A 'dragon king' so they say. I wouldn't say we are comrades."

"My motives were not my own. I ask your forgiveness for my deception."

His humility shocked me, but I couldn't help but admire it.

"Why hide in the Order at all?" Jesse helped Maddie back to the couch before positioning himself beside her. "What business does a dragon have with the Knights?"

"Didn't you ever wonder what happened to the dragons that were chained and sent away? Didn't you ever wonder where they ended up?"

"No. I can't say that I did."

Axel straightened his shirt. "It was easy to take those dragons and enslave them to the Shadows. No one was looking for them."

"You were building an army..."

"One I now intend to set free."

Simeon collapsed into a chair and Samara brought him food as he spoke. "Oh? Tell me, *dragon king*, how are two displaced royals, a rogue, his soulmate, a Knight, and a pregnant woman going to set free an army of dragons enslaved to dark magic?" He shifted in his seat, settling deep in the cushion. "This should be good."

Axel crossed his arms over his chest. "I need the Heart of the Sea, the Heart of the Mountain, two rogues, and the sword."

Simeon laughed. "I see one Heart of the Sea resting in our High Queen's chest, and one rogue. How exactly do you plan on getting the rest of it?"

"I need to find the Mountain Queen first."

"Jenna?" I whispered. "Jenna died. I saw it myself."

"What?" Jesse leaned forward. "Jenna...is dead? I know we haven't heard from...oh god..."

"She's not dead." Axel said sharply. "Not yet."

"What do you mean, she's not dead? I saw her die. You were there...You..."

He lifted his brow. "I what? Please continue."

I glanced between him and Simeon. "You...are you saying you did whatever you did to Simeon to Jenna? Are you telling me that she is alive?"

He nodded. "But we need to find her. Fast."

I didn't hesitate. I ran from the room, heading for the sea. My heart ached and I didn't know what to believe. I dove beneath the waters of my precious ocean and held myself there. Did I dare to hope? Was it possible that she was still alive?

My tears mixed with the sea and an iron fist clamped on my chest, squeezing until I couldn't stand the pressure. I hovered between shifting and drowning, not yet ready to face the world. My emotions came tumbling out of me into the waters. Blue flames flashed around me as I released each one.

A hand wrapped around my arm and brought me to the surface. I sputtered and coughed trying to clear my lungs.

"Heavens, Zale. What was that?"

"She's alive? And you knew?" I slapped my hand on Axel's chest and sent a blast of fire sending him back to the beach.

I prowled toward him through the waves. "You knew she was alive. You knew what she is to me, and this is the first you thought to mention it? She is my cousin. My family. I thought you killed her!" I released the waters and they covered him. I kept the waves in place, pinning him down and releasing my anger.

Then the waters split in a white flash. Axel stood with the waters parted and crossed his arms over his chest. "Are you finished?"

I sent the waves crashing toward him with the force from the stone in my chest, but they were held back by his magic. How was he able to resist the Heart of the Sea?

With a flick of my wrist, I released the waters and they receded off the beach. I marched up to him and clenched my fists as I glared. "You better talk quick, and then we are leaving."

His silver eyes stared into mine. "What do you want to know?"

Chapter Forty

Zale

"Tell me everything. Start at the beginning. Who are your parents?"

"I don't know."

I scoffed. "Really? Of course you would say that."

"Zale. You misunderstand. I was born a dragon. I was born before the binding."

"Before the binding?"

"Yes. The binding weakened me. I'm not sure if that was the intention of the clans or if they even realized my existence. I can't remember. I do know that the moment I could, I cut my cords, all of them, and disappeared. My mind was confused when I was bound in this form. It's not meant to hold the magic inside me."

"You cut them on purpose?"

"I didn't know who could see them. I didn't know I was the only one. At least until Simeon."

"And Jenna. She's still alive? You're sure?"

He stepped closer and put his hands on my shoulders. "I need her. She had better be alive still. Trust me. Please, Zale."

I stepped back from his reach. "Axel, this is all a lot to take in. And...it means that you couldn't control your actions. It means...I made a mistake cutting our cord."

"No. Zale, it woke me up."

We stared at each other on the beach. I allowed myself to see him in a new light. If he was telling me the truth, not only was his story tragic...he truly was the Dragon King.

He could save them all. He could unite the clans, which is what I had dreamed about for some time.

Axel held his hand out to me. "Come. Let's go see if this rogue can take us to your cousin. I'm eager to have this war behind us."

A thousand questions about how he planned to fight the Shadows filled my mind. I pushed them to the side and put my hand in his, my heart pounding in my chest. The heat from his hand burned itself into my memory as we walked back up the hill.

Before we reached the cottage, Axel stopped. "Will you give me a chance, princess? A chance to show you who I really am?"

I wanted to correct his words. I was the High Queen, but he grinned and his eyes twinkled with mischief. Was he...teasing?

"Save Jenna. Then I will give you a chance."

"A real chance, Zale. No holding back."

"We don't have a soulmate cord—"

"I don't care. I'll save the Mountain Queen. I was going to anyway, but I want you to try."

I stared in those silver eyes, wondering what he was thinking. He was so much a mystery to me. The thought of opening myself up to anyone right now frightened me. What if he were lying?

"I see your mind turning over everything. All I'm asking is for you to stop fighting and to try."

Giving him the slightest nod, I kept my face stone, trying to keep my thoughts hidden. He raised our joined hands and kissed my knuckles.

"Thank you, Zale. You don't know what that means to me."

He glanced over my face once more before pulling me to the cottage. All eyes focused on him when he pushed the door open. Axel wasted no time.

"Simeon, are you able to locate the Mountain Queen? We need to travel by portal to her as quickly as we are able."

"I can find her. Why should I?" Simeon glared at Axel.

"She will certainly die without my intervention."

"I could go and zap her heart like you did mine. Why do I even need *you*?"

"You have your secrets, rogue, but so do I. You will not be able to wake her. No one can but me. That was how I could guarantee her safety."

Simeon rose and faced Axel. "You did this to her."

"As a precaution. Will you help or hinder me, dragon? I don't have time for games."

Simeon's eyes darted to mine. He raised a brow. I gave him the smallest of nods. I didn't completely trust Axel, but if he was telling the truth, he could save Jenna.

He threw his hands up and stomped over to Samara. "Come on, darling. Apparently, we are going to have a little reunion party."

Samara's white and orange flames created the portal in the living room. Jesse moved Maddie to Samara's side. Simeon whispered something to Samara, and she nodded. Axel took my hand again and we approached the portal.

Simeon eyed our joined hands and then grinned at Axel. "If you think I woke up grumpy, I can't wait to see Jenna lay you out on your ass."

"Lead the way, dragon." Axel nodded to the portal.

Simeon and Samara walked into the fiery archway with Jesse and Maddie holding onto them. Axel stepped through, his hand holding mine. I inhaled sharply and the strange magic pressed in on all sides. My lungs burned and I couldn't stop the iron clamp that constricted around my chest.

Axel sent white flames around me, warming my body and easing the discomfort. Our eyes met and I wanted to get lost in his silver gaze, but I cleared my throat and focused on the light at the end of the portal.

We walked through the navy tunnel and relief flooded me when we emerged on the other side. At least until I realized we were deep inside a mountain, far from my precious sea.

"Simeon, you better have a good reason for bringing him here."

Kipp stepped out of the darkness, his arms lit with white and red flames—a shield prepared for battle.

Simeon waved his hand and marched past Kipp. "Ask Zale. Something about saving Jenna."

Relief crashed into me. Jenna was still alive because her soulmate stood before me. I left Axel's side, crossing the distance to stand before Kipp.

"Where is she? We can save her."

"No. He's not getting anywhere near her," Kipp growled, his eyes never leaving Axel.

"He can save her. I freed him from the Shadows. He saved Simeon. Please, Kipp. Take us to her."

Kipp glanced at Simeon. "Is what she says true?"

"It is. Although I still don't trust him."

Kipp lowered his flames. "She is weak. I've been giving her as much energy through the cord as possible...but..."

Axel came and stood at my side. "Take us to her."

Chapter Forty-One

Zale

W e followed behind Kipp through the mountain tunnels. He often glanced over his shoulder at Axel.

"Where are the rest of Mountain clan?" I wondered how many remained.

"They are gathered close by. They...are already mourning the Mountain Queen. I brought her here. Looking for a way to heal her."

"There is much magic here in the mountain." Axel studied the walls as we walked.

"I should hope so. The Heart of the Mountain was forged here. I thought it would save her."

Kipp lifted his hand and the red and white flames lit our way. He stopped in front of a tapestry and pulled it back to reveal a cave. As I stepped inside, foreign magic pressed in on all sides, threatening to suffocate me. It seemed as if the mountain did not welcome the sea. Axel moved around me to the pallet where Jenna lay.

Her dark hair was splayed on the pillow around her head. Her chest did not rise or fall. I had never seen her so still. She did not move at all. If Kipp were not walking among us, I would believe her to be dead.

We all waited to see if the Dragon King could do what he said he would.

He closed his eyes and hovered his hand over her chest. When he opened his eyes, they glowed with white flames. The fire spiraled down his arms and crashed into her body, seeming to tear open her very flesh.

Kipp cried out, but Simeon and Samara blocked his path.

Jesse's hand rested on his gun. He stepped up to my side. "He better know what he's doing."

"I think we can all agree that he will die if he doesn't fix this."

I watched with morbid curiosity. The fire flowed in Jenna's veins and illuminated her skin, stitching and healing as it moved.

Her eyes flew open. She released a bolt of flames into Axel's chest, sending him crashing into the wall of the cave. I put myself between the warring dragons and the humans. Samara noticed my move and snatched Maddie's hand, dragging her from the room. Jesse stayed on the edge of the cave, his weapon drawn.

"You stole the Heart of the Mountain from me!" Jenna fired flames into Axel's chest again as he rose. "You trapped me in my own mind!"

"It was necessary," Axel choked out.

"Necessary?" Jenna kicked his solar plexus. "It's a shame I can't kill you. I'll have fun trying though."

I moved to send my smoke into the room, but Axel lifted his hand, shaking his head. Did he know my intention?

"A lot has gone into keeping you alive, little dragon. I would hate to undo that now."

Jenna scoffed and tilted her head. "You wanna fight? Fine. I'm ready for you this time. No tricks." She raised her hands and released the flames, but instead of knocking him off guard, Axel caught them in his hand.

Simeon attacked. I watched in horror at the intensity of the rogue flames.

Axel caught the stream of fire and the cord between Simeon and Jenna illuminated the cave. The red and green strands wrapped around each other over and over as it stretched from one chest to the other. White flames lit the triangle of rogue dragons, and something happened—some sort of communication or understanding that only they could hear.

When Axel released the flames and all was quiet in the room again, my eyes darted around, waiting for the next attack.

It never came.

"You can tell no one," Axel began. "This plan relies on our stealth and keeping everyone in the dark. Share with your soulmates, but in secret. Can you promise me this?"

The air in the room simmered with tension.

Simeon crossed his arms over his chest and nodded.

Jenna glanced at Kipp and remained silent.

"Jenna, I need your word."

She marched up to Axel and crossed her arms over her chest. "I will agree to this. Once it's done, I want nothing to do with you."

Axel nodded. "I will honor that."

Simeon left, no doubt to find Samara. Jenna took Kipp's hand and Jesse followed them out of the cave as well, leaving us alone.

I clasped my hands together in front of myself. "That was quite the show."

"They do not trust me." Axel ran his hand through his hair. "I don't know that they ever will."

"No. I don't think that they will. What did you need from them?"

Axel raised a brow. "It's a secret." His lips curved the slightest at the edge, betraying a smirk.

"Oh? I thought you were sharing secrets with soulmates?"

Axel's face broke into a wide grin. "You admit that you are still mine?"

A shiver spread down my body from his words. "I didn't say that exactly."

"If you were my soulmate, I would not hesitate to share everything with you."

"That seems like extortion."

"It is the truth, Zale. So tell me, are you willing to give me a chance?"

I took a deep breath in and held it. Pondering the options I had, I decided to give a little. Maybe the information would help me with Sea clan. I released the breath and allowed myself to return his smile.

"I told you I would try."

Chapter Forty-Two

Zale

"Where are we going?"

Axel pressed his hand against my lower back as we walked. "Back to the sea. Your clan needs you."

"Wait. I'm not going without speaking with Jenna first."

He paused his walking, and his silver eyes scanned my face. "I am anxious to speak with you. We need privacy since our cord has been destroyed."

"What do you mean?"

"Joined soulmates can speak to each other through their cord. Emotions. Words. Intentions."

"And what you have to say is so secretive that you cannot whisper it?"

He pressed his hand on my back and continued walking. "No. We will need the sea to speak for us."

"I need to see Jenna."

Axel pointed me down a tunnel. "I will wait here. They are through there, princess."

"You...aren't coming?"

"They will not appreciate my presence. Go. Speak with your cousin. Then we need to return to the sea."

I glanced between him and the tunnel, wondering if I should insist. It was beginning to be exhausting to try and read his every intention.

"Go," he nodded his head down the corridor. "I'll be here."

My fingers laced together as I clasped my hands, walking down the tunnel. The walkway opened into a common area where my cousin rested against her soulmate. Her eyes darted to me as I approached, and she rose to greet me.

"Zale, what are you doing with him?"

"Let me see you first." I put my hands on her cheeks. Magic from the sea flowed from me and into her, restoring her body. "I thought you were dead," I whispered.

"I don't understand what he did to me. One minute we were fighting, the next I was trapped inside my mind and unable to move."

"And now? Now what do you think of the Dragon King?"

Her blue eyes darkened. "I would love to be able to kill him. That is not on the table. We need him to defeat the Shadows."

"I have to return with him. I need to gather Sea clan."

Jenna nodded once and pulled me into her chest for a hug. After all these years and her ferocious nature, I was still shocked when her humanity showed through.

When she released me, I turned to Kipp. "There were two Mountain dragons that escaped Shadowkeep with me. I understand one of them is a friend of yours. Marcos? Has he arrived?"

"Marcos? Marcos died with Desmond, Zale."

I shook my head. "You're mistaken. He...saved me in the prison. He's been there a long time."

"Marcos is alive? He's been..."

I could tell Kipp warred with his own emotions at the news.

"He can tell you himself when he arrives. He is a valued friend of mine. Please let me know when he arrives."

Jenna wrapped her arms around Kipp's waist. "We will. Safe travels."

"Tell Simeon...tell him I will call for him soon."

Jenna nodded and I retraced my steps up the tunnel. A sudden apprehension grabbed a hold of me, thinking that Axel might have had an ulterior motive for staying behind. My steps hurried and I breathed a sigh of relief when he stood leaning against the wall of the tunnel.

"Miss me?" He grinned.

"Hardly. It was barely a moment." I walked past him in the direction we previously were headed. He caught up to me and placed his hand on my back.

Axel leaned closer and whispered in my ear. "I missed you, princess."

I darted my eyes to his before facing forward again. His words threatened to tear down the walls around my heart.

"Now, where are we going? Specifically."

"We will go back to Medney Island and collect the Sea dragons we left behind. Then, there is a place I know on the northern coast of Alaska that will serve our purposes."

"And when will you be sharing your secrets?"

"In good time. And as soon as possible."

He led me through the tunnels until we arrived in a portal room. I looked around for a Mountain dragon but there were none.

Axel approached the mirror. He sent his white flames into the words of the old script. The portal activated and the surface rippled like water.

I raised my brow at his action.

Axel's eyes twinkled. "I have many talents." He held his hand out palm up. "Ready?"

I eyed his hand and the portal again.

"If it were my preference, I would carry you through. I don't know that you will allow me that pleasure yet."

"No. I will not." I placed my hand in his. "I am quite capable of a simple task such as walking."

"What a pity." He smiled as he squeezed my hand. Wrapping white flames around me, he tugged me forward.

When we entered the portal, pressure formed around my chest, but it was not as bad as the other times. I clenched my jaw and focused on putting one foot in front of the other.

The light at the end of the tunnel grew larger as we approached. When we crossed the threshold of the portal, I breathed in the ocean air and smiled.

On the beach of Medney, I ran to the waves and let the ocean greet me. Standing in the surf, I communicated with Ramos and Tamil to head to the northern coast of Alaska—the sea carrying my words to them.

Axel entered the water and stood at my side.

"Are you ready to spill your secrets?"

"Are you ready to choose me as your soulmate?"

"Choose?"

"Yes. We no longer have a cord, but we can still choose each other."

I faced the ocean. "You ask a lot of me, Axel."

He took my hand, drawing my eyes back to his. "I know. Forgive me. I'm impatient."

I pulled back my hand. "Are you ready to leave?"

He cleared his throat. "Yes."

"Lead the way."

Chapter Forty-Three

Axel

I n all my years, I had never met anyone quite like Zale.

I likely never would again.

It was a shame she didn't trust me.

But part of her wanted to.

Was it the part of her soul that spoke to mine? I truly hoped so.

I dove beneath the surface of the waves and shifted, shedding the human form I found so uncomfortable in exchange for my wings and my tail and my scales.

Zale shifted behind me and I found the currents with ease, the sea speaking to me as she always had.

There was so much about my soulmate I didn't understand, but I wanted to.

She was strong and regal in every word she spoke.

And she was good. Far too good for me.

But what made her smile? What of my soul spoke to hers? What drove her to make decisions? What made her blush? What made her flood with desire?

No matter how long I watched her in Shadowkeep or how often I touched her, she remained a mystery to me. One that I was desperate to solve.

There were pieces of herself that she kept hidden. I doubted she would ever willingly share those parts of herself. I would have to learn by observing her.

The water ran over my scales as I pushed my tail back and forth in the sea, reminding me of the comforts the ocean held.

I let the water soak into my body and soul, restoring and reconnecting me to this part of myself.

The ocean greeted me as I acknowledged this part of my magic. Sea magic ran deep in my veins but had long been suppressed by the Shadows. The ocean reminded me of all the times before the binding when I traveled in its rivers.

The ocean held many memories—all water did.

Did I dare to look at them?

Every time Zale ran to the sea, it would be held in this water's memories. Every time she greeted it with her smile. Every time she greeted it with tears.

Before I thought better of it, I reached out with the deep magic that rested in my soul and asked the sea to show me.

Show me every time my soulmate came to you.

The images swam through my mind in a stream of flashes. Zale's entire childhood with Keani and Ada and Simeon ran through my vision. She grew in strength and wisdom. I saw her release ceremony when the sea granted her the deep magic. Her eyes darted around to the High King and her father frequently during this time.

Then I heard the sea calling her to wander. She ignored this calling for many years.

And when she finally wandered, her face became sad.

Something changed.

I saw her, bruised and bloody, coming to the water to be restored.

My blood boiled within my body. Flames threated to erupt from my chest.

Who was she sparring with?

Who was treating her like this?

I saw her race against her rogue cousin. She pulled herself up short, allowing Jenna to win. And...the next memory was one of her bruised and bloodied again, coming to the ocean.

Zale raced through the ocean to this place and that, always on a mission. Always saving someone.

Had her whole life been about serving those around her?

I saw her free the first dragon from the Shadows and I was never more proud of my soulmate than in that moment.

She held the Shadows in her hand, her eyes wide, and lit them with flames.

Her countenance changed after that. She was...like stone. Even when she came to the sea, broken, with blood dripping down her face, she held no expression. But with every Shadow she pulled from dragons, she smiled. Only the slightest one, but she did.

The next memory confused and shook my soul.

Zale stood in the waves and allowed her father to lock golden chains around her wrists. She did not release the waters on him. She did not break herself free. She followed behind, her chin held high as he yanked her from the ocean.

Who did he think he was? He dared to shackle *my* soulmate?

White flames left my mouth as I roared. My body hummed with the violence of my magic.

He should thank the ocean that he was already dead at my hands. I wanted to peel his skin from his body and cut pieces from him until he screamed loud enough to wake the dead.

Then a horrifying thought crossed my mind. Was he the reason she was bloodied when she ran to the sea? Was it her own father?

I had to know.

This couldn't wait. I needed the name of the person who hurt her.

I changed our course and brought us to a secluded beach. I shifted and walked up onto the sand, my hands shaking with my rage.

"Is this the place?"

I turned and took her in.

"Who hurt you?"

Her brows pinched.

"Hurt me?"

I closed the distance between us. "Tell me, Zale. Who put those bruises on your body all those years?"

"How—"

"Tell. Me."

Chapter Forty-Four

Zale

H urt me?

What was he talking about?

"How—"

"Tell. Me."

His silver eyes held fire behind them as he clenched his fists.

I pinched my lips together, wondering how to answer him.

"It was a long time ago."

"Zale. Tell me."

What was he after? And how did he know I had been hurt?

"My father and my grandfather. Both of whom are dead at your hands."

He studied my eyes and then turned from me, his hand on his mouth. Axel stood there with his back to me for so long, I was unsure what to do next.

When he finally turned back, he put his hands on my face. "I am...so sorry."

"Sorry?"

"My soulmate should have been celebrated her entire life. Balance to my power in every way, you are a miracle."

The intensity of his gaze and his sincerity froze my breath. His words struck me in my soul. Never had anyone held me in such high regard.

"No one has the right to harm you. I swear to you, Zale. No one who harms you from this moment on will live. Whether you choose me or not."

He kissed my forehead, holding his lips there for longer than he should. I closed my eyes, soaking in the moment. Was it possible that he saw me? I wrapped my fingers around his wrists, feeling his pulse quicken with my touch. I wanted so badly to believe him. Could I?

I pulled in a breath and his scent surrounded me. It spoke to some deep part of me and, for once, I wanted to listen.

All my life, I watered myself down for those around me. I became a version of myself I needed to be to survive. My soul wanted to wander. My soul wanted to be free and never have to live in a cage. My soul wanted...

I squeezed my fingers tighter around his wrists and tilted my chin up to press my lips to his. I leaned against him and lost myself in him. A flash of emotions flew through me, striking me with their intensity, and I pulled back. Longing, pain, love, acceptance, joy, sadness and desire mixed together inside of me. The world shifted on its axis, and nothing was the same as it was before that moment.

Could the magic of our souls still recognize and long for each other?

Axel's gray eyes searched mine—waiting.

Could I trust him? Did it matter?

A little trust could go a long way.

"Do...do you feel..."

Axel's thumbs stroked my cheeks. "You feel your soul responding to mine. I feel it too."

I wanted to trust him.

A part of my mind begged me to trust him.

But it was too much.

I stepped back away from him and cleared my throat. "Can you tell me what you shared with Jenna and Simeon now?"

Strategy and planning were easier than soulmates who may or may not still be soulmates.

To his credit, Axel's face did not betray any disappointment or anger. He gave me a small smile and took my hand, leading me back into the ocean.

"Here is as good a place as any. I would rather not do this near any of the other dragons anyway."

"What are we doing?"

"Didn't you learn that the deep parts of the ocean can speak to you?"

I tugged my hand from his in the waves. "What do you mean?"

He turned and faced me, his face astonished. "You don't know? Zale, you have the deep magic and the Heart of the Sea. Who taught you about your magic?"

"Keani taught me."

"Ah. She would not be one to teach you this part then. She likely believed you heard the waves as she did. She was...always wild."

"Explain. What do you mean?"

"You and I share deep magic from the sea. We will be able to communicate under the waves."

"Why would Keani never mention this?"

"Zale, Keani was from my time. And now that I know the power that you hold from the Heart of the Sea, I guess she was tasked with guarding it right after the binding. It would explain her nature."

It was true. Only those with deep magic could hold the Heart of the Sea. Keani was the only one other than myself with the deep magic.

And now Axel. The revelation dawned on me.

"You can hold the Heart of the Sea."

Axel raised a brow. "And?"

"Why didn't you take it from me in Shadowkeep? Why do you not take it from me now?"

He held his hand out again. "Come, princess. Let me answer your questions under the waves."

More trust. He always asked for more.

Chapter Forty-Five

Zale

I followed him into the water.

When I shed my human form and followed him through the sea, I heard his voice in my mind. The intimacy was undeniable, and I regretted cutting our cord even more. We would not even have the chance for this in the future.

'The water can channel our thoughts.'

'I know this. It is how I command my clan.'

'Do they ever speak to you this way?'

When I considered, they did not. How did I not realize that my dragons only heard me one way in the ocean? It was how it had always been.

'No.'

'I want you to listen and understand. Please, Zale?'

'Tell me what you need to say.'

'The only way to defeat the Shadows is to dissolve the clans. We have to unite them under one ruler.'

'I wanted this too. The clans won't be happy with it.'

'It doesn't matter. It's the only way.'

'And you are the only one who can do this?'

'I am.'

'How do you plan to do this?'

'The same way that Celeste planned to use me—find the sword and bind the Heart of the Sea with the Heart of the Mountain. She gave up on this plan when we couldn't get the Heart of the Sea from you.'

'This is the third time I have heard of this sword. What is it?'

'It's what was used at the binding, but it is much, much older than that.'

'What would a dragon need with a sword?'

'I didn't say it belonged to the dragons. It belonged to the Knights. And it can only be wielded by a Knight of the Order.'

My mind immediately thought of Jesse and the visions I had of him. Was it all connected? 'Then how does it work? Humans have nothing to do with dragons and our magic.'

'The clans were formed while we were dragons only. Two brothers wanted to claim the Dragon King title for their own, so the legend goes. They consulted a sorcerer who suggested that they divide magic between them, each taking domain over one. The brothers agreed and the sorcerer formed a sword capable of wielding magic. He split the dragon's magic, and the brothers went their separate ways. After it was done, the sorcerer needed to ensure that the sword wouldn't be used for evil. So he charmed it so that only a Knight of the Order could wield it, knowing that the dragons would have to use a human, and that in and of itself would be almost impossible. After he charmed the sword, he spoke to the sea and asked her to hold it in her depths. He asked her to protect it.'

'Charming story.'

'You don't believe me.'

'Perhaps. I want to believe you, but I do not know these legends. What do they have to do with the Shadows? Or the Heart of the Sea?'

'I'll show you.'

Visions pushed through my mind. I recognized the deep magic, but the visions were not my own. They flashed in a moment, and it was over.

I analyzed how the vision showed Axel forging the stones to the sword. How the sword cut through the Shadows and sent them hissing into the night. I watched how Axel, Simeon, and Jenna held Celeste in the center of their flames and how the Shadows were released.

It would work if these visions were correct.

And it would change everything.

Celeste was the source of the Shadows. Somehow, she controlled them and used them to bind dragons to herself.

Once the source of the Shadows was defeated, the dragons enslaved to the dark magic would be free.

It was everything I wanted.

I didn't care about ruling. It was what my clan needed but it wasn't something I chose.

I wanted the dragons free. I wanted to see an end to the Shadows.

And I wanted to wander.

Wander.

The voice echoed in my mind almost as if in response to my thoughts.

Axel led us through the frigid waters until we reached a small town. He traveled just beyond it before shifting and walking to the beach.

Did he have any reason to lie? I wanted to trust him, but...

But what?

Had he lied to me?

No. Since he was stripped of the Shadows, he had not lied. He had only been honest. Maybe not forthcoming, but he answered honestly.

In fact, he had never lied to me. Even when he was manipulated by the Shadows.

He had made no move to harm me since I removed the Shadows.

I touched my lips as I waded through the waves. My soul stirred inside me, urging me forward—urging me to him.

What did I have to lose?

He could have harmed me. He could have stolen the Heart of the Sea. He could have deceived me.

But he didn't.

He could have what was left of my fractured heart.

"Axel?"

He turned and his silver eyes found mine. I closed the distance between us, stopping a few inches from touching him. Indecision warred inside me, but in the end, I decided I was all in. I raised my eyes and gathered all my courage.

"Kiss me."

Chapter Forty-Six

Zale

His eyes twinkled and the corners of his mouth lifted. What was he thinking?

He took my hand and began walking up the beach. My heart dropped and tears burned the back of my throat. Was he...turning me down? Had he changed his mind?

"Axel..."

"Hmm?"

He kept walking but didn't look back at me.

"Axel...can we forget..."

He spun and pulled me against his chest. "Zale, if you are ready to trust me, I'm not going to kiss you on the icy waterfront of Alaska. Trust me. I will want more than to kiss you."

His words warmed my heart and I nodded. "Okay."

Axel took my hand again and brought me to an empty house. It was close enough to the shore, but tucked away behind a grove of trees.

"What is this place?"

"Somewhere I secured shortly after you cut the cord."

He opened the front door—no lock. Not that the Dragon King would need a lock on his door.

"It was a failsafe. Somewhere secluded where I could go to heal and regroup if needed. I did not know how pulling the Shadows would affect me. Still, my memories are not completely restored."

Axel shut the door behind me and sent flames into the giant hearth, lighting the wood inside. He pulled me flush to his chest and traced his fingers down my face. I leaned against his embrace.

"I won't be able to stop at a kiss, Zale. My soul has longed for you my entire existence. Tell me you're ready."

Anticipation fluttered inside me and I wanted to pull back, but I wanted to see if this could be more. If I opened myself up to the possibility of being loved, would he love me?

"I'm ready. Please, Axel, kiss me."

He claimed my lips with his, parting them and sweeping his tongue against mine. Every movement he made elicited a reaction from my body, and I moaned. He grazed his hand up my spine and threaded his fingers in the hair at the nape of my neck. I pressed my hands against his chest and dug my fingers into his muscles. He gripped my hair and tilted my head to his pleasure.

It was indescribable, the way his soul spoke to mine without words. Nothing before or after would ever compare.

My heart skipped a beat when he swept my legs out from under me, cradling me in his arms. I gripped his shirt, and he carried me through the doorway to a bedroom.

Axel laid me out on the bed and stripped the clothes from my body. His fingers trailed across my skin leaving chills in their path. I glanced at the black bedposts that stretched to the ceiling, but he brought my attention back to him when he covered my body with his. His tongue traced a line from my neck down my sternum and he peppered kisses over my breasts before pulling one peak into his mouth.

I arched against him and gripped his shoulders, holding him closer. Heat flooded my core and I needed him. I needed more.

He ran his hands over my thighs, and I pulled the shirt from his chest. "Get rid of these." It was taking too long. I ached for his skin against mine.

Axel smiled against me. "Gladly, my queen."

I watched him and my body heated more with his words than any action he had done so far. He shed his clothes, and I took my time scanning his body—perfect in every way.

"Queen?"

Axel smirked and leaned over me on the bed, pressing a quick kiss to my mouth. "Queen. *My* queen."

Before I could respond he wrapped his hands under my thighs and pulled me closer to the end of the bed. He threw my legs over each of his shoulders as he knelt before me.

"Axel—"

All my thoughts stopped as his tongue found my center. He held me steady and I arched my back, unable to stay still. My moans turned to screams and heat built low in my belly. Axel never let up his ministrations and I tugged on his hair, pulling him closer.

When the waves of pleasure rolled through me, his name fell from my lips and I closed my eyes. The emotions built and the pressure against my soul begged for more of him.

Axel kissed his way back up my body and I wrapped my legs around his waist. He lined himself up with my core and entered me with one thrust. Fully seated inside me, I dug my fingers in his back, holding him in place.

He stretched me perfectly. Nothing could be better than this moment—fully connected to my soulmate.

For he was mine and I was his.

It didn't matter that there was not a cord binding me to him. Our souls were tied together, despite my poor choices.

Then he moved. His hips rocking back and forth, testing how I would respond. I opened my eyes and locked onto his. The silver orbs beckoned me to drown in their depths, and for the first time, I wanted to. Everything around me faded and drowned out. There were no problems. There was no war. There was nothing but him.

I ran my hands over his chest and scraped my nails down his back. He leaned down and kissed me as his speed quickened. The familiar heat began to build in my core again. Axel increased his pace, and I moaned as he took me over the edge with him.

We held each other, basking in the new comfort of this relationship. How could I have doubted him? Why had I denied myself this for so long?

My soul hummed, fully satisfied. Piece by piece, my fractured heart began to see a future. One where I could be whole again.

The heat of his body next to mine was something I could see myself loving forever. Waking next to Axel, my spent body draped across his, was something I didn't know I had craved.

Wander.

The voice echoed louder in my head than it had in the past.

"It's getting louder," Axel murmured, his voice thick with sleep.

"It is. It's getting harder to resist."

He pulled me closer, running his hand up the back of my thigh. "Maybe you aren't supposed to resist it."

I lifted my head. "I have my clan to consider. We need to gather them. We have a war to win."

He grinned and lifted a brow. "We?"

"Mmm. Yes." I kissed his lips. "We."

I rose and pulled my clothes back on.

"I had a thought." Axel sat on the side of the bed.

"Yes?"

"The sword was given to the sea, and you hold the Heart of the Sea."

"I do."

He rose and drew me back into his arms. "What if this voice is the sea calling you to the sword? Calling us both there."

I looked up into his eyes, waiting and studying. No one, not even Lance, had encouraged me to wander. Other than Carl, but he was an enigma of his own. A part of me wanted to pull away, to avoid allowing Axel into the potentially vulnerable parts of me, but I shoved down the thoughts. I was choosing to believe him. To...trust.

"Do you think I should follow it?"

"I think *we* should follow it."

"Hmm. I have my clan to think about."

"Go with me to the voice. You can summon the clan after we retrieve the sword and have hope to show them."

I had never shared the burden of my decision-making with any other. Should I trust him? Should I allow him to influence me?

Pulling out of his arms, I went to the hearth, studying the flames. What he was suggesting made good sense. I folded my hands in front of myself and chewed on my lip.

"Zale?"

I met his eyes over my shoulder. His eyes darkened and he raised a brow. "Trust me? This is the best way."

"I'm not used to being influenced. I make decisions."

"After what we shared you still doubt?"

"One night of passion can't build trust."

I regretted the words even as they spilled from my lips.

Axel strode toward me and took my shoulders in his hands. He turned me to him and lifted my chin, holding my gaze. "We shared more than one night of passion, and you know it. Say it. Say that you know there is more between us."

Tears burned the back of my throat.

"I need you to say it, Zale. I'm desperate for the words."

My words were hardly a whisper. Why were they so hard to force out?

"I know it."

His hand drifted to my throat, trailing his fingers across my pulse. "You can struggle. We both will. But do not lie to yourself. I certainly won't let you lie to me."

Axel's hand tightened around my neck ever so slightly and he dropped his lips to mine. The kiss was hard but brief. With our mouths almost touching, he spoke straight to my soul. "You are mine, and I am yours. Cord or not."

He dropped his hand and disappeared into the other room.

Tears snaked down my face and I held my hands to my chest. How was he so right and almost too much at the same time?

And he was mine.

Chapter Forty-Seven

Zale

The Dragon King was mine.

The thought alone astounded me. We belonged to each other.

Not because of a cord. But because parts of our souls knew the other.

There wasn't time to dwell on the magnitude of this, or how it shifted my entire world.

We had a war to win.

Axel returned from one of the other rooms and wrapped a blanket around my shoulders. It was a small action that brought a smile to my face.

"Rest for a while longer. We can leave when you're ready."

I tugged the blanket closer but stood and faced him. "Axel. We should go. Now. I want this part to be over."

Wander.

I winced as the voice clamored in my mind—the insistence pressuring me to move.

He wrapped his arms around my waist and kissed me. "It seems we won't get any reprieve."

"Rulers rarely do."

Reaching up on my toes, I kissed his lips softly. "Let us go, then we can strategize how to win this war."

He took my hands in his, kissing them each. "As you wish, my queen."

My cheeks heated and warmth filled my abdomen. Was this what it would be like? To be cherished every day? Did that future await me?

I pushed the thoughts aside. We had to find the source of the voice and hopefully the sword. I tucked the blanket away and stored up these memories in my heart. This moment of peace in a timeline of disasters was more precious to me than gold.

We left the house and trekked back to the beach. I waded into the frigid waves, diving beneath their depths to shift.

Wander.

The voice pulled me with the currents.

I sensed Axel shifting and following behind me.

Wander. North.

North? We were north. How much further north did we have to go?

Ice formed on the surface of the ocean and still the voice pulled me.

Wander.

The more I listened, the more the command forced my direction.

The fires of my dragon heated my scales and I moved with the streams in the ocean.

Wander.

I pushed through the surface of the sea, breaking the ice and spreading my wings in the air. The slopes of ice climbed up out of the ocean and between two peaks rested a cave. It was illuminated with green and blue lights, reflecting into the night time sky.

Here.

The voice seemed closer now. I shifted as I dropped to the hardened ice before the cave, my feet landing with perfect balance. Axel joined me at my side. Whatever waited for me in the cave, we were in this together.

"Are you ready?" He held his hand out to me.

I placed my hand in his and gave him a tentative smile. It refreshed me to allow him close, like a balm to my battered soul.

"Yes."

As we approached the cave, ice broke behind me. I spun and flames spiraled down my arms as my gold tattoos flared to life.

Behind us, a green dragon shot up out of the ocean through the ice. It spread its wings and roared into the night. Axel's flames covered his body. Just as he was about to shift, I put my hand on his arm.

"Wait."

The green dragon landed with a gust of air before us. His green flames spiraled around him, and he shifted, a twinkle in his eye.

"My queen," Carl bowed as he spoke.

I crossed the ice and embraced my friend before holding his shoulders and examining him. "Carl, how did you find me?"

He shook his head. "I did not know you were here, Majesty. The sea called to me with a voice like the wind. I had no choice but to come." He glanced behind me at Axel and dipped his head again. "Your Highness. Good to see you free of the Shadows as well."

My eyes bounced back and forth between them. "You...acknowledge him?"

Carl's sea-green eyes bored into mine. "He has always been the Dragon King. That has never changed."

Axel clapped the dragon's shoulder and pulled me into his side. "Let us hope that others see it as you do."

"They must, if we are to win this war against the Shadows."

"Hmm, you are correct, seer. Let us hope your visions can help us."

"Seer?" I glanced between them.

Carl grinned. "I have many secrets, Your Highness. The sea shows me many things, including the Dragon King's enslavement to the Shadows and when the savior set him free."

I brushed aside the praise. It was the Heart of the Sea and not me that cleansed the dragons. I only followed the calling. "There haven't been seers in Sea clan for many generations. My grandfather brought them all to him. When he was displeased with their visions...he slaughtered them."

"Are you sure that there are not many? A seer knows a dragon's intentions from what they see. Perhaps, they are waiting."

I looked to Axel, hoping he knew something of this. "Waiting? For what exactly?"

"The next age. The coming of the Dragon King."

Axel pressed against the small of my back and guided me forward. "That future can not exist unless we find the sword. Come. We need to find the voice."

The entrance of the cave dripped with ice. Stalactites fell from the ceiling of the cave ominously. The air was thicker here, heavier than it should be. Light bounced all around the walls, moving like visions. Deep magic greeted me, welcoming me into its depths.

I stepped forward and Axel's hand dropped from my back. I looked at him and he and Carl stood frozen behind me.

"Why have you stopped?"

His silver eyes scanned mine. "I cannot go forward."

Chapter Forty-Eight

Zale

W*ander.*

The voice called to me from inside the cave, beckoning me closer.

Giving him a small smile, I moved back to his arms. I reached up and kissed his lips. "Don't worry. I'll be right back."

Carl cleared his throat and averted his eyes.

I squeezed Axel's hand before moving further into the cave.

Light illuminated the walls. Blues and greens and purples all sped along the ice as I moved further into the depths of the cave. The hairs on my arms rose and my tattoos became visible on my skin. Anticipation hummed through me. Why had the voice called?

Deep magic rested here.

My magic.

The magic of the sea.

The stone pulsed in my chest, and I pressed forward, following the voice, following the light. I turned the winding passage and stopped at the wall of ice before me. Old script was carved into the ice in the pattern of a door. It looked like Mountain magic with their portals.

A light in the darkness.

I glanced around. Why was the voice calling me here? To a wall of ice?

No. There had to be more.

Blue fire spiraled down my arms and I lit the wall of ice ablaze. The ice steamed and hissed but broke through, opening to a small chamber.

There was more weight to the air as I stepped into the chamber, reminding me of the in-between. The lights moved slowly in every color around the icy walls. I moved with caution into the center of the chamber. This place was sacred, but I didn't understand why. At least not until I looked up.

A sword wrapped in a black scabbard hung suspended in the ice, waiting to fall.

I lifted my hand to the sword above me and prepared to release my fire into the ice and free it.

"Wait." The voice of my aunt echoed off the walls.

I spun, looking for Keani but not seeing her.

"Where are you?"

A figure moved on the other side of the ice wall. "I cannot come to you. Not like I used to."

"Why are you here? What is this place?"

"You do not know it?"

"Should I?"

Keani sighed. Her voice sounded weak and tired rather than the normal commanding way she spoke to me in the past. "It is the Heart of the Sea."

I touched the stone under my skin. "I have the Heart of the Sea."

"You have the *stone*. And you have brought it home."

I touched the ice where the figure moved, hardly able to make out the shape of her eyes.

"I'm here because the voice called me. And I'm here for the sword, Keani."

"I couldn't let you do it. Not until you knew the truth."

Keani's words sent more ice through my veins than was surrounding me. "What truth? What do you mean?"

My eyes darted around the cave, no longer certain I was safe.

"The sea will only allow you to release the sword in exchange for something else. Something precious. A life."

My stomach dropped.

"A...a life?"

"The sorcerer's sword is valued by many. To protect it, the sea will only grant it in exchange for a life. Yours."

"Mine?"

"I have spent many years trying to change this moment, but I cannot. Since my very first vision of you standing here, I worked to alter it. I am so sorry I failed you."

My mind raced and my flames ran down my arms in response to my fear. What was she asking? What was she saying? In the end, I let my flames dissipate. It didn't matter the price. Dragons needed that sword. Axel needed it to free them.

"What do I have to do?"

"Zale...you would offer yourself to the sea, in exchange for the sword. She will keep you in her embrace, like the sword."

I glanced at the sword suspended in ice. "A...a cage. A cage of ice? For how long?"

"I...I do not know. I'm sorry. The ancestors...they are displeased. Even now the Mountain King works against me to seal your fate."

The Mountain King? The last Mountain King was...Desmond, Jenna's father. Did she mean Desmond? Was he one of the ancestors? I clasped my hands in front of myself and turned to look at the sword.

If I wanted my clan to have a chance, Axel needed that sword. And he needed the Heart of the Sea inside my chest.

If I wanted to free dragons from the enslavement of the Shadows...there was no choice.

Fire blazed all around me. My flames mixed with those from the Heart of the Sea. I prayed that Axel would be able to move past the boundary once I freed the sword.

I squeezed my eyes shut and whispered to the icy walls as my heart shattered once again. "Please forgive me. Save them."

I raised my hand and sent the flames into the ice that held the sword. In moments, the heavy weapon fell into my hand, and I held it to the light.

Pulling the stone from my chest, I locked it in place in the sword. The magic spiraled around us, and I gasped at the display.

Something changed and shifted magic. I knew it in my very core.

My limbs grew heavy as the sea pulled on my body.

I laid the sword on the floor of the cave.

My breathing became deeper, and my heart began to slow.

Fear settled in my soul. Fear of this cage.

It would be better to die than to be left here.

As my heart slowed to a stop and the ice rose up to surround me, I hoped Axel knew how deeply I truly cared for him and trusted him to save me.

Chapter Forty-Nine

Axel

The faintest of rumbles trembled the ice below my feet. Magic shifted in the air.

I reached my arm forward and the barrier that held me back was gone.

Something was wrong. I needed to get to her.

"Come with me."

Carl followed me, and my strides ate up the distance between my heart and hers. I knew that something wasn't right. It was too...still around me.

The cavern lit up with lights of the northern sky, responding to my entrance. On the floor lay the sword, with the blue Heart of the Sea bound to the hilt.

But that wasn't what drew my eyes.

It was the tomb.

A tomb of ice, where the other half of my soul rested.

I pushed the sword away and held my hands to the ice, heating it with my flames.

"That won't work."

"It has to."

The dragon placed his hand on my shoulder. "Your Majesty, your flames won't free her. She couldn't have been taken by the sea against her will. I foresaw this."

Beneath the ice, a distorted vision of my Zale broke my heart. I couldn't reach her...touch her.

I rose to my feet and sent a cascade of flames all around the cavern as I roared—my body hovering the line between shifting.

Steam from the heat filled the room and a vision of Zale stopped me in my place.

She laid her hand against the ice wall and spoke as she closed her eyes.

"Please forgive me. Save them."

My love. My *queen*.

Why?

Why would she ask this of me?

I had only found her for a moment. A time so brief, it would never quell my thirst for her. No amount of time would.

My breathing slowed and I took the sword in my hand, examining the way the Heart of the Sea sat in the hilt. The stone remained fused to the sword no matter which way I turned it.

"Do you think she lives?"

I turned and looked at my love, frozen and trapped in the ice. "She must." Rising to my feet I walked to the wall of ice that separated us from the in-between. My flames allowed me to see the figures on the other side. The ancestors watched my every move. *He* watched me. The one that vowed I would pay for my part in the death of his love.

"If she does not live, I will not stop until I find her and return her to my side. I will tear down every boundary. Every barrier between our world and the one after."

Whispers from the ancestors echoed around the cavern.

They should be afraid. My threat was very real.

The sea may require a sacrifice, but it was they who decided which side of the barrier she remained on. I would not stop until my soulmate was at my side once more.

I was the Dragon King.

Nothing would stand in my way.

With a parting glare at the ice, I strapped the sword to my belt and turned to Carl.

"She trusted you?"

He nodded. "She did."

"There is something I must do. Can I trust you with her safety?"

The dragon grinned viciously as he pulled something from under his shirt. He took the pouch and opened it to me, showing a variety of gems. "I knew I was collecting these for a reason."

Dragging my hand over the stones, I embedded them with as much of my magic as they could hold. "That should help. I don't know what the ancestors want with her, but do not let them come through the barrier to retrieve her."

"I'll protect her with my life."

I held his shoulder. "I'm counting on it."

It was not within my power to walk away without trying one more time to free Zale. I fired my flames at the ice, but it held steady. She was so beautiful, even trapped as she was. I laid my hand on the ice and infused my flames with my intentions. Perhaps they would reach her through the water. Perhaps not.

Before I could talk myself out of it, I walked away and out of the caverns.

The pressure on my mind to return to her side increased with every step I took.

This wasn't right.

She should be with me.

Always.

Clenching my jaw, I vowed to myself that she would be freed.

My queen would be at my side once more.

Nothing would stand in my way—especially *him.*

But, one problem at a time.

Now was the time to gather the clans.

Chapter Fifty

The faintest of rumbles trembled the ice below my feet. Magic shifted in the air.

I reached my arm forward and the barrier that held me back was gone.

Something was wrong. I needed to get to her.

"Come with me."

Carl followed me, and my strides ate up the distance between my heart and hers. I knew that something wasn't right. It was too...still around me.

The cavern lit up with lights of the northern sky, responding to my entrance. On the floor lay the sword, with the blue Heart of the Sea bound to the hilt.

But that wasn't what drew my eyes.

It was the tomb.

A tomb of ice, where the other half of my soul rested.

I pushed the sword away and held my hands to the ice, heating it with my flames.

"That won't work."

"It has to."

The dragon placed his hand on my shoulder. "Your Majesty, your flames won't free her. She couldn't have been taken by the sea against her will. I foresaw this."

Beneath the ice, a distorted vision of my Zale broke my heart. I couldn't reach her...touch her.

I rose to my feet and sent a cascade of flames all around the cavern as I roared—my body hovering the line between shifting.

Steam from the heat filled the room and a vision of Zale stopped me in my place.

She laid her hand against the ice wall and spoke as she closed her eyes.

"Please forgive me. Save them."

My love. My *queen.*

Why?

Why would she ask this of me?

I had only found her for a moment. A time so brief, it would never quell my thirst for her. No amount of time would.

My breathing slowed and I took the sword in my hand, examining the way the Heart of the Sea sat in the hilt. The stone remained fused to the sword no matter which way I turned it.

"Do you think she lives?"

I turned and looked at my love, frozen and trapped in the ice. "She must." Rising to my feet I walked to the wall of ice that separated us from the in-between. My flames allowed me to see the figures on the other side. The ancestors watched my every move. *He* watched me. The one that vowed I would pay for my part in the death of his love.

"If she does not live, I will not stop until I find her and return her to my side. I will tear down every boundary. Every barrier between our world and the one after."

Whispers from the ancestors echoed around the cavern.

They should be afraid. My threat was very real.

The sea may require a sacrifice, but it was they who decided which side of the barrier she remained on. I would not stop until my soulmate was at my side once more.

I was the Dragon King.

Nothing would stand in my way.

With a parting glare at the ice, I strapped the sword to my belt and turned to Carl.

"She trusted you?"

He nodded. "She did."

"There is something I must do. Can I trust you with her safety?"

The dragon grinned viciously as he pulled something from under his shirt. He took the pouch and opened it to me, showing a variety of gems. "I knew I was collecting these for a reason."

Dragging my hand over the stones, I embedded them with as much of my magic as they could hold. "That should help. I don't know what the ancestors want with her, but do not let them come through the barrier to retrieve her."

"I'll protect her with my life."

I held his shoulder. "I'm counting on it."

It was not within my power to walk away without trying one more time to free Zale. I fired my flames at the ice, but it held steady. She was so beautiful, even trapped as she was. I laid my hand on the ice and infused my flames with my intentions. Perhaps they would reach her through the water. Perhaps not.

Before I could talk myself out of it, I walked away and out of the caverns.

The pressure on my mind to return to her side increased with every step I took.

This wasn't right.

She should be with me.

Always.

Clenching my jaw, I vowed to myself that she would be freed.

My queen would be at my side once more.

Nothing would stand in my way—especially *him.*

But, one problem at a time.

Now was the time to gather the clans.

Chapter Fifty-One

Axel

Every step away from the ice weighed my body down more.

If only our cord were still intact, I would know for sure that she was alive. I could support her.

I pushed the thought to the side and created a portal to Mountain clan. The magic drifted through my veins with lazy ease. Magic was the easy part though. Facing the clans without Zale at my side would be nearly impossible.

They would have to trust me.

They knew nothing of me except from my captivity in the Shadows.

Tearing the veil between space, I stepped into the portal and marched forward. On the other side, dragons waited with flames ready. My lips twitched. They had no idea what I was capable of, but they would know. Soon.

I stepped through the shimmering mirror and scanned the faces. Jenna wasn't here.

"Take me to the rogue queen."

Mountain warriors filed in around me as we walked through the tunnels of the sacred stronghold. The old script jumped out around me as we moved. Likely, these dragons didn't know or couldn't see the sacred writing. It spoke of the heat of the earth and how the magic of the mountain came from the rivers of fire, something I knew in the deep recesses of my mind. Mountain magic ran hot, their tempers were fierce. They were lucky to have inherited such a bold queen.

"Where is my cousin?"

Jenna's voice echoed around the room as I entered. She stood with her dark hair cascading over her shoulders and her blue eyes flaring with flames. The Mountain Queen held her head high and her stance ready to attack. I marveled at the perfect combination of her parents. Keani's eyes and wild nature with Desmond's chin and powerful leadership.

I regretted my part in their deaths. Under the Shadows, I used my position at the Order to negotiate a peace treaty, only to turn around and betray them both at Celeste's request. I only failed to locate and exterminate their child, who Keani had hidden away.

Celeste was right to not want their child to live.

Jenna was a force in and of her own right—her power rivaling my own, but not exceeding it.

"I need to speak with you."

She spread her arms wide, the knives at her hips visible. "Speak. I'm here."

"Privately. Please."

She considered my request before giving a subtle nod to her clan. The dragons filed out of the room, leaving me standing with Jenna. Her soulmate stepped to her side and crossed his arms over his chest.

"Where is Zale? Why is she not with you?"

I pulled the sword from my belt and laid it on the table between us. "She is with the sea, trapped under the ice."

Jenna's eyes flared with flames, and she reached her hand out to touch the sword. She pulled her hand back and lifted her chin.

"Then go get her."

"It's not that easy. The ancestors are displeased. And the sea required a sacrifice to retrieve the sword."

Her eyes studied mine, but I held her gaze. She needed to trust me. She didn't want to, but we both needed it.

"Why would the sea demand her life?"

I tapped the sword. "This. This is not something that should exist. The sorcerer made sure that it was well protected."

"And this is the only way? To defeat the Shadows?"

I nodded. "We have to unite the clans."

Her soulmate growled behind her. "That will not be easy."

"It will be easier with your support."

"What you're asking for will change magic for every dragon. It...changes everything."

"That is what we need. Something that will change everything."

Please believe me. Make this easier, Mountain Queen.

Jenna's blue eyes narrowed before she moved to the entrance of the room. "Marcos."

Part of my mind relaxed when the dragon entered. He scanned the room, looking for Zale, no doubt.

"Where is the High Queen?"

I held the sword up to him. "She sacrificed herself for this. She remains trapped with the sea."

The older dragon's eyes scanned the sword. He traced the place where the Heart of the Sea rested. Then he moved his fingers over the opening that waited for the Heart of the Mountain.

"So it does exist..."

Jenna stepped up between us. "Marcos, you will travel with Kipp. Go to this place where the *Dragon King* says Zale is. Confirm his story."

I raised a brow at the young ruler. "You doubt me?"

"Would you trust me? If the roles were reversed?"

"Depends. The question you should be asking is do you need to trust me to gain what you need from me?"

"Hmm." Jenna turned to her soulmate and placed a kiss on his lips. He wrapped his arms around her, and I yearned to do the same to Zale. My time with my queen was too brief.

Soon. Soon that would be me again.

"Where is this place, Your Majesty?"

"North. Almost as far north as you can travel. I have left a Sea dragon named Carl to guard her." I placed my hand on Marcos's temple and showed him the place where my love rested.

Kipp clapped Marcos on the shoulder and the two left for the portals. Jenna stepped out of the room and whispered to one of her guards.

"What will you do? Once the clans are united?"

"Free our kind from the Shadows."

"I mean after. There won't be any returning the magic once it's set free. The clans will not exist any longer."

"No. They will not."

"Do you mean to lead us?"

I hesitated. It was a question that I pondered often since being freed. It was my birthright, but did I want it? Was I the right one to lead? "I mean to find Zale and free her from the ocean and the ancestors if I must."

"You aren't thinking like a king."

"I bear the title but I haven't been leading our kind."

Jenna placed her hand on her hip. "My clan. I need your assurance that you will not forget them before I do this. They are my priority."

"How could I forget them? They have half of my heart, mind and soul."

"You are bound to the sea. I have never seen a dragon embody the sea like Zale."

"She does. She is magnificent."

Silence filled the room. Jenna appeared to tolerate me. Perhaps there was hope.

"What do we have here? A displaced Dragon King? Where is Zale?"

Behind us, Simeon stood in the doorway. The rogue raised his brow, studying me as if he were trying to decide whether he should fight me or not. My patience was thin. It would not go well for anyone in this mountain if they opposed me.

Jesse pushed past Simeon. "Is that what I think it is?"

Jenna handed her brother the sword. "It is."

Jesse pulled it from the scabbard and tested the feel of it. "It's almost perfect, but it's slightly off balance."

"It is missing the Heart of the Mountain." I pointed to the empty space where the stone would rest.

"Too bad you were better with guns than swords at the academy." Jenna grinned at Jesse.

"Too bad you turned out to be a dragon, J. You do love your blades."

Simeon snatched it from Jesse's hand. "This is a legend. You can't possibly be thinking about joining the clans."

"This is our only chance. Zale gave herself in exchange for this."

"What?"

"Where is she?"

"Trapped by the ocean in ice."

Simeon stormed out of the room. "Not for long. Damn ocean doesn't get to decide her destiny."

"You think I didn't try?" I marched after him.

He spun and sent flames into my chest. I absorbed the blow and he snarled. "If you tried, then she would be here, *Dragon King*."

"It is not only the sea. The ancestors keep her there."

"They do not decide for us."

"No. They do not. But Zale believed that this was the only way. That this was how we freed our kind from the Shadows. And I will do everything in my power to make that future a reality."

I let the white flames spiral down my chest and arms, toying with the flames in my hand. "And when I'm done, I'll go and get my queen."

Chapter Fifty-Two

Axel

W e waited.

It took too long.

Too much time away from her.

The dragons stewed and simmered, waiting to find out if I spoke the truth.

Finally, Kipp and Marcos returned to the chamber deep within the mountain.

Kipp nodded to Jenna. "He speaks the truth."

"Will you help me now? We have wasted too much time."

Jenna rose and her eyes danced about the room as the smallest grin appeared on her face. "Mountain clan will join you. It's time we reclaimed the Heart."

"Good. I need to gather Sea clan."

"From what we know, those that remain are scattered in every direction."

"They will come."

My skin itched and I wanted to leave this place. To shift. To make happen what needed to happen. The longer I stayed here the longer Zale was trapped beneath the ice and my soul could not bear it.

"Don't you need this?" Jesse called after me, holding the sword and scabbard up.

"It is not for me to use."

"It's not complete though."

I turned and crossed my arms over my chest. "Knight. You test my patience. I will complete it when I have the Heart of the Mountain. It is for *you*."

"You want me to keep it, Axel?"

With a sigh, I put my hand on Jesse's shoulder. "Call the Order. We need all the help we can get. This is yours until I can put the Heart of the Mountain in its hilt. After you destroy the Shadows, I will return it to the sea."

"I need to tell the general."

"No. This is for you. Only you. I don't trust that Celeste isn't up to her old games with the Order. She may still have spies in their ranks. I can't risk the sword falling to the Shadows."

Jenna appeared at his side. "Where do you want us to join you?"

I closed my eyes and reached out to all the pieces of my magic, searching. The Shadows were gathering, but not at Shadowkeep.

"Firestorm. That's where Celeste and the Shadows are."

"Firestorm? It was destroyed. I expected her to be at Shadowkeep."

This was taking too much time, and I had no patience for gentleness.

"Celeste is your aunt. Your grandfather made her with a witch after the binding. She will see the fortress as hers."

"Um, excuse me? What?" Jenna shook her head. "I have two crazy aunts?"

"It would appear so."

"Bad luck, J." Jesse bumped his shoulder against Jenna's arm.

"I must go." The itch was scouring my entire body. I needed to shift. The magic thrummed inside me, begging to be released.

"How will we know? When to come?"

I didn't stop. I didn't pause my gait. I needed to move. "You will know."

No portals for me this time. Celeste needed to know I was coming. Sea clan needed to know I was coming.

As soon as I could see the blue of the sky, I began to shift. Stretching my neck, I roared into the air. My wings snapped out and I flew down the mountain. I released white fire from my jaws as I reveled in the feel of the air on my scales.

The earth hardly changed in my life, but there was an edge to time that tickled the edges of my mind. Magic was changing.

The beginning of a new era.

Would I be part of it?

Could I save them?

Could I save her?

So much was crumbling down, and it would be so easy for any of us to slip away.

As I came to the sea, I dove beneath the waves and let my tears mix with the water. Tears for those we would lose. Tears that Zale was not at my side.

When the time for tears was done, I broke through the surface and stretched the ashy canopy of my dark wings completely, soaring above the water.

The Sea fortress came into sight—Firestorm. Celeste had been busy in my absence. The fortress was rebuilt and swarming with Shadows. How many traps had the witch laid for us?

Shadow dragons milled about the island, and I circled around it once before letting out a bellow.

I wanted her to know I was here.

Her time was almost up.

With one last dive, I lit flames to the trees that lined the fortress entrance before moving to where I would call Sea clan to me.

I shifted as I landed on the beach in the surf. I slammed my foot into the waves and sent a shock through the water. My magic pulsed out of me in ripples, calling them. Commanding them.

Come.

Deep magic pulsed through me, and I sent flames into the waves.

Come to me.

Lifting my hands to the sea, I sent one last blast of flames into the water.

Come now, Sea clan.

And then I waited.

They would come.

They had to.

Chapter Fifty-Three

Zale

T he in-between was colder than it should have been.

Probably because I was trapped in ice.

I shivered and pushed aside that particular fact. Being buried alive under the ice was not something I wanted to think about.

Everything was foggy. It hadn't always been this foggy. But I had only been there in my dreams before. Now...

Now, I wasn't even sure if I were still alive. When the sea claimed me, I felt my body shudder as my heart came to a stop. How long could my soul linger in the in-between? And how long would my body last without my soul?

"Walk with me, Zale."

"No." I turned so I could ignore Keani.

"This was the only way."

"The only way? My life was stolen from me. You put me in a cage."

Keani came to my side and placed her hand on my shoulder. "I didn't do this to you. You chose this cage. I worked to prevent this future."

"What choice did I have? Condemn thousands of dragons to darkness or save myself?" I scoffed and brushed her hand off my shoulder. "That is no choice."

I walked down the beach and my heart ached for my sea. For the warmth of the sand and the playful waves. For the healing powers that brought me comfort. This...This dreamland didn't hold the true sea. It was so painful, especially when I carried her Heart in my chest for so long.

And my soul also ached for him. I didn't need a cord to know that Axel was my other half. Separated from him made it impossible to think clearly.

"You have a choice now, Zale."

"Ha!" I kept walking.

"You do."

I turned and lit my flames into my aunt. She caught them without difficulty and sent them into the false ocean. Anger burned a pit in my belly. I wanted to shift, but that didn't happen in the in-between.

"Zale. I don't want to see you trapped. You can choose to cross over. You could see your mom. Your friends. It is a good place."

"My life is not over."

"What life? What kind of life do you have if you wait?"

"One that is full. One with my soulmate. Axel will save them. Then he will save me."

"And if he doesn't?"

"He will."

Keani placed her hands on my shoulders again. "You can wander in the afterlife. Nothing will stop you. Nothing will hold you back."

"That is not the life I want."

Keani dropped her hands from my shoulders and crossed her arms. "We do not always get what we want, Zale. I walked away from my love. From my child. From my clan. My family. I gave it all up, for a chance. For the future of all dragons."

"I know that! Your choices are not my choices. I'm choosing to believe. I'm choosing to wait. To give Axel a chance."

Keani turned her eyes out to the sea. "You will not be able to choose how long your body will be able to wait."

I sat in the sand and let the waves play with my hand. It was true. I knew that my body would not survive forever without my soul. The longer they were separated, the harder it would be to go back. All I could do was hold out...as long as I could. Give Axel a chance at the future we both wanted. "I know," I whispered.

Keani sat next to me. "You have done well in this life. You should be proud."

The voice behind me forced my spine to straighten. "Proud? She freed the Dragon King. He deserved to die with the Shadows."

Standing in the dunes with his arms crossed over his chest, his dark eyes narrowed on me. This dragon dripped with power. I knew his face even though it had been many years since his death.

"He deserved to die?" I rose to my feet and let my flames flow down my arms. "Tell me why, Mountain King."

Keani touched my shoulder and she raised her head to Desmond. "There is a chance. There still is a chance for dragons."

"Does that negate the ones he slaughtered?"

It was strange. I knew Desmond, but only as the Mountain King. Seeing him with my aunt, I looked at him in a new light. He loved Keani. That much was clear now. There was so much of Jenna's fierce nature radiating off him.

"Our time was over, Desmond. There was no path around that where Jenna would live. The only way to keep her safe was the path we chose."

"The one you chose, Keani."

"Will you always dwell in the past, Des? That time is over. The new one is coming."

He marched up and Keani met him a few steps from me. He looked at me over her shoulder. Keani put her hands on his face and drew his eyes back to hers.

"Zale has nothing to do with this."

"She is his soulmate. He deserves to feel what I did..."

"But what does Zale deserve? Des, see this clearly."

The Mountain King put his hands around her wrists and kissed her palm. "This is not over my love. We may not agree, but you must allow me this."

He dropped her hands and walked back up the dunes.

"Don't make me choose," Keani whispered after him.

I swallowed down my own emotions. How tragic for my aunt. Her soulmate was from another clan. She chose a difficult path, all to give dragons a chance. To give Jenna a chance.

But what did that mean for me?

Would the Mountain King keep me here? Would he stop me from returning? All for his revenge?

"Give him time, Zale. He will see things my way." Keani put her hand on my shoulder and then wandered down the beach away from me.

I watched the hazy sun begin to dip below the horizon, trying not to fall asleep.

There were many mysteries in the in-between, but I knew one thing for certain. The moment I fell asleep, my choice would be stolen from me, and I would cross to the afterlife, no matter what I wanted.

Chapter Fifty-Four

Axel

They came.

It didn't matter that their numbers were few.

It didn't matter that they didn't want to.

They responded to the sea, and the sea wanted this war with the Shadows to end.

So she brought them to me.

I walked the beach and studied each of them. What could I say to them that would earn their trust? Their loyalty?

Is that what I needed?

No.

I only needed them to follow me. To fight against Celeste and the Shadows.

"Sea clan. I called you to me so we can end this war."

"You are one of them!" The older dragon spat in the sand and flashed green flames.

"I am free of the Shadows."

"No one escapes the Shadows." Another dragon stepped forward.

"I am free because of your High Queen. She freed me. She saved me from the Shadows."

The waves crashed on the beach as murmurs rose up from the dragons. The pit in my stomach grew bigger. They needed to believe me. How could I make them see?

A small dragon with sharp eyes stepped forward. "My name is Eden. Tiamat saved me from the Shadows. She goes by another name here. Zale."

My heart rejoiced that one of those saved was still alive.

Ramos and Tamil stepped forward. "We were trapped in Shadowkeep. The High Queen saved us. And him."

"You saw this?"

"Yes. It is true."

"Where is the High Queen? Why did she not call us herself?"

I stepped among them, drawing their attention back to me. "She is with the sea."

One of the dragons stepped forward. "Does she live?"

"I believe so."

"Why should we follow you?"

There it was. The one question I feared. The one I wasn't sure I knew the answer to.

Sending white flames down my arms, I shot them into the air. I made sure the display was grand and full of power. Power is something all dragons could follow.

"I am the Dragon King. I can stop the witch. I can stop the Shadows."

I lowered my arm. "I won't ask you to follow me forever. I am asking you to honor your queen's sacrifice. That you follow me to this one end—to defeat the Shadows."

One by one, they nodded their agreement. It was more than I could have asked for in a dozen centuries. They honored their queen's sacrifice this way. It was more a testament to Zale than any words that I said.

Touching the ground, I let the Mountain clan know that they were needed. A pulse of my magic entered the earth, and I knew it would reach them. The mountain would call them to me.

I scanned the horizon and watched as dragons flew over Firestorm. The dark magic of the Shadows threatened to choke me. I felt its slithering presence and steeled myself against it. I was not a slave to the Shadows any longer. Fear served no place for me here and they could not reclaim me without my consent. I may have been fooled once, but I wouldn't make the same mistake twice.

A portal sparked on the beach and Mountain clan filed out of the portal to join us.

"That took less time than I imagined." Jenna scanned the horizon as she approached. "That's where the Shadows are?"

I nodded.

Simeon stood at Jenna's side. "Wonder how many there are? Samara said there were thousands of dragons enslaved."

"It's true. Where is your soulmate?"

"Mind your own business, *Dragon King.*" Simeon marched forward and stood in the waves with his arms crossed.

"Don't mind him. He gets pissy when he isn't with her. She's with my wife and daughter," Jesse said as he joined us.

"Your daughter?"

He smiled widely. "Sarah Hope Daly. She's the most beautiful thing I've ever seen. But I couldn't leave her and Maddie unprotected."

I clapped my hand on his shoulder. "Congratulations, Jesse." I looked back at Firestorm and wished we didn't need a Knight. No human should be caught up in this war. "I wish it were different."

"Me too. I called the Order. They should be sending Knights within the hour. Let's get this over with, shall we?" He grinned and went to stand with Kipp.

I motioned to the dragons to move forward and walked into the waves. My mind wavered for only a moment, but I remembered what was at stake. Even if we walked along the edge of a sword, ready to tip one way or the other, we must go forward.

My mind resolved, I said the words that gave me strength.

"It ends here. The time of the Shadows is over."

Chapter Fifty-Five

Axel

S he was ready for us. I would expect nothing less.

The wards around Firestorm were powerful.

Not powerful enough to resist me.

I flew over the fortress as dragons battled around us. The Shadows filtered through the air and threatened to make it impossible to see.

There.

I dove and clawed at the gems embedded in the walls of the fortress. The magic prevented me from crossing the boundary into the fortress and it needed to come down.

We had to get inside.

Step one, collect the Heart of the Mountain.

Last time I saw it, Celeste wore it around her neck. That made things more complicated—but not impossible.

The thought of how she trapped me for so long spurred me on. She came to me so long ago, and I felt compassion for her story. Celeste was rejected by her mother's coven. She was not welcome among the dragons of Sea clan. So she asked for something so simple. Something so easy that I didn't even realize I had been tricked until it was too late.

She asked for just a bit of my blood to protect herself. She didn't want to die. She didn't want to be a victim to the magical forces in her life, and so I took pity on her. I still didn't know how she had found me. That should have been my first clue. When she slit my palm, she slit hers right after and the magic locked around me, drifting into my vessels and heart in a matter of moments.

Anger fueled my motions as I dug my talons into the stone wall, tearing more and more gems from it and releasing the magic. She would regret that day, I would make sure of it.

Fire bore into my back and I roared.

Turning, I snapped my jaws at the closest dragon. One of the rogues dove and pinned the dragon to the sand beside me before closing its jaws around the dragon's neck. The bones crunched and snapped and the Shadow dragon fell limp with death.

One more of our kind lost.

I returned to tearing out the gems. We needed to use portals to bring Jesse to the fortress when it was time. Once the barriers were down, we would flood into the fortress and find the witch.

But the portals were for step two.

Back to step one.

I felt the snap of magic break with the final gem I tore from the walls. Shifting, I moved through the crevice I had made in the stone. I looked up and down the halls wondering where to look.

Where was she?

She was smart. I wasn't as familiar with this fortress as I was with Shadowkeep. She could be anywhere.

For as smart as she was though, she was still vain.

A grin tickled my lips.

She would be in the throne room.

Shadow dragons met me as soon as I turned into the main corridor. I did my best to disarm them and not kill them. The point of this war was to save them.

But they needed to get out of my way.

I sent a bolt of white flames through the hall, clearing a path from me to the throne room. Shadows moved about the hall, heralding my arrival and whizzing past me.

I threw open the doors of the throne room and Celeste sat on the throne in a red dress, her legs kicked up over the side as she played with the Shadows in one hand. The sight of her made bile rise in my throat. I wanted to be washed clean of every memory I ever had with her.

"Axel. I've missed you."

"Give me the Heart of the Mountain, Celeste."

She spun on the throne and placed her feet on the floor. Her fingers drummed on the arms and she tilted her head. "No foreplay this time?"

"I'm afraid I'm no longer interested. The Heart. Now."

Celeste leaned forward so that the necklace hovered over her cleavage. "Come get it."

I'll need your help now.

She had something up her sleeve. I marched forward and climbed the stairs to the throne. I reached my hand out for the necklace but the Shadows flashed and snapped at my hand.

"Did you think it would be that simple?" Celeste put her foot on my chest as I still stood on the steps below her. "You will regret the side you chose, Dragon King."

"I doubt it."

She pushed me back with her heel and sent Shadows spiraling in my direction, pushing me across the room. I shielded my face with my flames.

"You coming to me does make things simpler. I would have hated to track you down."

Celeste pulled a black jagged dagger from her side, the blade swirling with Shadows.

"You like it? I made another, since you broke the tip of my other one."

"You broke the blade yourself when you buried it in my chest."

Celeste shrugged. "Details." She played with the tip of the blade and let a drop of blood drip from her finger. "Red always was my favorite color."

Our magic was locked, neither gaining control over the other. The Shadows pushed back on my flames, trying to extinguish them.

"The Heart of the Mountain. I'll be taking that now."

"You think you can pressure me? You think that I'll just hand it over? I worked hard for this. It's mine."

"Actually, it's mine." Jenna marched into the room with Simeon at her side.

"Oh good. Everyone in one spot. It really does make my job so much easier." Celeste pointed the dagger at Jenna as she spoke.

Shadows relented their battle with my flames and began to spiral into the room. They danced around Celeste and buried the light, making it nearly impossible to see.

Simeon sent flames into the witch and she smacked them away with her dagger.

"Hmm. That's new." He glanced at me.

Attack on my count. Go for the Heart of the Mountain. We will destroy her after.

Simeon and Jenna nodded.

One...Two...Three.

Each of us sent flames at the witch. She pulled the Shadows closer to herself and deflected each of the flames.

With the speed of a rogue, Jenna ran close enough to pull the necklace from Celeste's neck. She was fast—faster than either Simeon or me. The witch couldn't hold us off and escape from Jenna at the same time.

Jenna darted behind us while Simeon and I continued to fire on Celeste.

Don't kill her. Not yet.

More Shadows joined Celeste. Other than the light from our flames, the room had become completely void, giving it an ominous appearance. My throat threatened to close up. It reminded me of when the Shadows controlled my mind. They would choke out my thoughts and hide memories from me.

"Call them, Jenna. Get them here."

I looked over my shoulder. Jenna held the Heart of the Mountain tight in her fist. She glanced between me and Celeste, Shadows darting over her face.

"Jenna?"

She didn't respond. She only stared at the Heart of the Mountain with Shadows closing in around her, whispering.

My stomach clenched. Now was not the time for surprises. We were so close.

So close to ending the reign of Shadows.

Chapter Fifty-Six

Axel

"Jenna!"

She stared at the Heart of the Mountain as the Shadows spun around her, partially hiding her from view.

Simeon glanced over his shoulder, still holding fire to Celeste. "Jenna! Pay attention!"

Something snapped in her mind. She glared at Simeon.

"Call them here. Bring us the sword!" My voice wasn't as sure as I would like, but we didn't have much time. We had to move.

Jenna formed a portal, clenching the stone in her fist. Simeon covered her and pushed back the Shadows while I continued to fire on the witch.

Celeste was desperate. There was something dangerous in her eyes. She knew.

We both did.

It was the reason that we tried to prevent Jenna from being born all those years ago. One rogue was dangerous. Two rogues could ignite a war. But three? Three could change history.

A triangle of rogues could destroy magic, even magic as dark and potent as the Shadows.

Kipp brought Jesse through the portal, their eyes taking in the scene around us. Each of them moved with purpose before the Knight handed me the sword.

"Make it whole."

Kipp began to cover Jenna and Simeon fired on the witch.

"The heart? Jenna!"

She glanced at the stone in her hand. When she looked up, her eyes snagged on Jesse, and she tossed me the stone.

My soul breathed a sigh of relief. I did not want to have to fight her this day.

Pulling on the deepest magic of the mountain, I fused the stone with the sword. The earth trembled and magic filled the air, making it hum. The joined hearts flashed around the sword and pierced through the Shadows, the light bouncing in every direction.

I shoved the sword back into Jesse's hands, and turned to find Jenna and Simeon.

Behind us, a roar ripped through the room and everything became utterly silent, until a white dragon thrashed her head and tail. Celeste had shifted—a last effort to evade what would happen next.

"Don't let her escape!"

Simeon grabbed the red and green cord between himself and Jenna, sending white flames along it. He prowled around her to the front of the dragon. We had to make the triangle and light the flames.

I ran straight at Celeste and dove under her belly. Sliding on the floor, I emerged behind her.

Now.

Both Jenna and Simeon fired their flames at me. I caught the fire and completed the triangle. White hot magic hissed as it began to destroy the Shadows. They hissed as they were pulled to the center of the triangle before they burned out of existence. Celeste opened her jaw and released fire at us, but they could not break through the rogue magic.

I struggled to hold on to the flames as our collective magic pushed the Shadows and Celeste down. Even with the power humming through me, my body stretched and begged to shift. I had to stay in this form. Holding on to the cords was the only way.

Shadow dragons fell around us as their dark magic was stripped from their souls. Some fell where they stood, others from the air. They moved slowly, some didn't move at all. Would they survive this?

"Jesse! Now!"

The Knight touched his sister's shoulder before he ducked under the flames and entered the center.

Celeste snapped at him and roared. She was unable to take flight, trapped by the triangle. That didn't make her any less deadly. She was still a dragon.

Jessed dove out of the way. He grunted when his arm touched the flames, and he rolled away. I shouted to him to watch his step.

The Shadows wrapped around his body, pulling his feet from him. He hacked at the dark magic and the sword split though with a flash. He jumped back to his feet.

Celeste whipped her tail, her serpentine body moving with incredible speed. Jesse jumped over it, barely in time. The Shadows reached out to grab him, but he twisted the blade and cut them off.

Back and forth they went as we destroyed more and more of the Shadows, but were helpless to intervene.

Then, there was an opening. Jesse dodged the snap of her jaws and brought the sword down across her neck. The blade, enchanted by the sorcerer, sliced through the scales and severed her head from her body. A flash of light broke around the room and dark blood spilled from the white dragon.

A snap of magic split the air, throwing us all from our feet.

Rubble from the fortress fell around us and light entered where the Shadows left. Smoke from our flames filled the air.

I pushed myself to my feet, looking at Simeon and Jenna. They pulled themselves up out of the debris. Jesse coughed and Jenna fought to reach him, wrapping him in a tight hug.

Simeon's pale green eyes locked onto mine. He raised a brow and gave the slightest nod.

I breathed a sigh of relief.

We did it.

The end of the Shadows.

Chapter Fifty-Seven

Axel

The dragons freed from the Shadows shuffled around Firestorm. Many were still disoriented from their time enslaved. I went to each of them, speaking to my fellow dragons. I wished with everything in myself that Zale was there at my side. She would have wanted to see our kind freed.

"Here."

I looked up to see Jesse holding the sword to me.

"This is yours."

My hand wrapped around the sword. "You fought well, Jesse."

"Good thing I spent a lot of time sparring with dragons."

"I'm indebted to you."

"The Dragon King is indebted to me?"

I held my hand out for him. "It's Axel."

He grinned and took it. "Still haven't gotten used to that."

"Go. You have a family waiting on you."

"I do. I'm the luckiest man in the world."

When Jesse left, I took the sword and walked to the sea. I studied the hilt where the Heart of the Sea and the Heart of the Mountain rested.

It wasn't safe to have these all together. This much power was too tempting for any dragon.

Zale, hold on for me just a bit longer. I'm coming.

Without saying goodbye, or explaining myself, I did what was in my nature.

I wandered.

The Dragon King was not meant to stay in one place for long.

The portal I used brought me to the sacred mountain. I wandered through the tunnels until I found the center. Molten lava rivers ran through the belly of the mountain. I pulled on my magic and forced the Heart of the Mountain from the hilt. I held the amber stone to the light. It was beautiful—a fierce topaz.

I tossed the stone into the lava, returning the magic back to the mountain.

Magic was already changing. This would ensure that the balance was restored. The clans were destroyed as they should be.

Without wasting any further time, I built a portal and walked through to the ice where I had left my queen. My soulmate.

"You're late."

Carl rose from the ice and pointed to the chamber where Zale rested. "She is barely holding on."

I rushed to the ice and put my hands on it, willing the fire to melt it.

When it wouldn't yield, I ripped the Heart of the Sea from the hilt of the sword.

"Is this what you want? Take it! Take everything! Just give her back to me!"

The sea reached through the ice and pulled its Heart down into the murky depths below.

"Take it! Take this cursed sword and give her back!"

I shook the sword in the air as I shouted. Figures moved behind the ice.

"They say she crossed to the other side." Carl laid his fingers on the icy wall. "They say...they will not release her.

"Like hell!"

I rose and sent a blast of my flames into the ice that separated me from the in-between. I wrapped the sword around my waist and moved to the entrance I had made.

"You won't be able to return."

I faced the older dragon. "I will. I am the Dragon King. They don't get to keep her. She gets a choice."

It wasn't even a question. I wasn't going to go through everything we went through and turn away because I might not return in the end. It would be worth it to make sure my soulmate was not abandoned.

I looked down the beach and she sat with her feet in the waves.

My heart pounded in my chest and relief washed over me. "Zale."

Somehow, she heard my whispered word over the waves. She turned her head and her eyes widened.

"Axel!" She jumped to her feet and ran to me. I dropped the sword to the sand and caught her as she launched herself at me. "I knew you would come."

"I will always come for you."

I laid my lips on hers, holding her hand to my chest. Was there anything better than having her next to me?

"We can't stay here." She pulled back and studied my eyes.

"No. I will follow you wherever you choose."

"Where I choose?"

"If you choose the afterlife, I will go with you there. If you go back to our lives, I will follow."

"Where I choose?"

"Yes, my queen. Where *you* choose. You are not trapped."

She looked out over the waves and then back to me.

"I want to go back."

"As you wish."

A strange magic vibrated the air, one I recognized from long ago.

"No one leaves."

Zale let her flames spiral down her chest and I glanced at the person I least wanted to see—the Mountain King.

"You don't get to decide, Desmond."

He crossed his arms over his chest. "I vowed that I would see you suffer. You are free to go back through, but she stays."

My anger burned at his words. "I did not come this far to leave without her."

I lifted my hand and fired flames into his chest. He sent them into the air as if he were batting away a fly. That shouldn't be possible.

"Your magic doesn't have dominion here. The ancestors rule here." Desmond prowled closer. "And I've been waiting for you to come."

The air turned thin and my breathing became labored.

"Axel." Zale took my hand, and I followed as she guided me further down the beach.

"Zale, I...I can't breathe."

"You have to go." Her eyes filled with tears. "They won't let you stay. They won't let you cross over."

"I'm not leaving without you."

She bit her lip and took my face in her hands. "I am so thankful for the time we had. And I'm so disheartened it wasn't longer."

"Don't do this."

She kissed me and I clung to her, desperate to be closer.

"Leave!" Desmond's voice commanded from down the beach.

My body was pulled from hers without my consent, drawing me back to the ice. "No! Zale!"

I reached for her, but she stepped away and my heart shattered. This wasn't our story. This wasn't how it was supposed to end.

As the magic forced me back through and sealed the ice in front of me, I roared. My flames did not disintegrate the wall. I pounded my fists on the wall.

Carl put his hand on my shoulder but I pushed him aside.

She was gone.

I laid my head against the wall and slid to my knees.

"There is still hope, Your Majesty."

"There...is no hope. Not without her."

This was where I would stay the rest of my days. I would remain here and wait until my endless days came to a close.

A flash of light from the other side of the ice bounced around the cavern.

"Move, Your Majesty!"

Carl pulled my body to the side as a blast broke through the ice.

Zale walked through the ice with the sorcerer's sword in her hand. She crossed the barrier and tossed the blade to the ground.

The sea released her and the ice melted away from her body.

She went to where her body rested and her soul returned to it. I ran to her, cradling her head to me. When her breathing finally began, I put my hands on her cheeks. Looking back at me, she studied my face with more adoration than I could hope to earn in a lifetime.

"It's over?"

"Yes, my love. It's over."

"They're really free?"

"We all are."

The End

About the author

An American fantasy and romance author, Leigh loves her family, a strong cup of coffee, and happily ever afters.

Mother to four wild boys and an ICU nurse on the side, she can usually be found in yoga pants or scrubs. (Aren't those the same things?)

When she isn't wrestling, refereeing, or loving on the boys, (or at the hospital) she can be found cuddled up with a fuzzy blanket, a bowl of popcorn, and a good book.

Also by Leigh

The Shadow Dragon Series
The Cord Between Us

The Pieces Around Us

The Stars Against Us

The Sword Above Us

The Melody Chronicles
Mist Guild Archives

The Twelfth Siren
A Cursed Covenant

Legends of Cheia with Teshelle Combs
Sever and Split

Tales of Ba'karan
Waking Flames

Connect with me

Want to keep up with the latest updates with my books? Join my Facebook group Leigh's Dream Lounge.

Follow me on Facebook at Leigh Fields

Follow me on Instagram @authorleighfields

Follow me on TikTok @authorleighfields

Support me on Patreon at Leigh Fields

Made in the USA
Columbia, SC
24 July 2024

38667874R00157